For more than forty years,
Yearling has been the leading name
in classic and award-winning literature
for young readers.

Yearling books feature children's
favorite authors and characters,
providing dynamic stories of adventure,
humor, history, mystery, and fantasy.

Trust Yearling paperbacks to entertain,
inspire, and promote the love of reading
in all children.

OTHER YEARLING BOOKS YOU WILL ENJOY

THE HERO, *Ron Woods*

THE IRON GIANT, *Ted Hughes*

JOSHUA T. BATES TAKES CHARGE, *Susan Shreve*

MR. TUCKET, *Gary Paulsen*

SPRING-HEELED JACK, *Philip Pullman*

BILLY HOOTEN: OWLBOY, *Thomas E. Sniegoski*

BILLY HOOTEN, OWLBOY: THE GIRL WITH
THE DESTRUCTO TOUCH, *Thomas E. Sniegoski*

Tremble at the Terror of Zis-Boom-Bah

by Thomas E. Sniegoski

illustrated by Eric Powell

A YEARLING BOOK

Published by Yearling, an imprint of Random House Children's Books
a division of Random House, Inc., New York
Sale of this book without a front cover may be unauthorized. If the book is coverless,
it may have been reported to the publisher as "unsold or destroyed" and neither
the author nor the publisher may have received payment for it.

Text copyright © 2008 by Thomas E. Sniegoski
Illustrations copyright © 2008 by Eric Powell

Visit us on the Web! www.randomhouse.com/kids

Educators and librarians, for a variety of teaching tools, visit us at
www.randomhouse.com/teachers

Library of Congress Cataloging-in-Publication Data is available upon request.
ISBN: 978-0-440-42236-5 (trade)—ISBN: 978-0-385-90544-2 (lib. bdg.)

Printed in the United States of America

August 2008

10 9 8 7 6 5 4 3 2 1

First Edition

For James Mignogna. Fighting the good fight.

ACKNOWLEDGMENTS

This book wouldn't have been possible without the love of my wife, LeeAnne, and the amazing typing skills of Mulder the Wonder Dog. I'm highly indebted to you both.

Special thanks bombarded with mutating gamma rays go out to Stephanie Lane, Christopher Golden, Dave "Is this supposed to be dripping?" Kraus, John and Jana, Harry and Hugo, Mike Mignola, Christine Mignola, Katie Mignola, Don Kramer, Greg Skopis, Pete Donaldson, Jon and Flo, Bob and Pat, Kim and Abby, Dan "The Lifesaver" Ouellette, Sheila Walker, Mom and Dad Sniegoski, Mom and Dad Fogg, Eric "I think I need more work" Powell, and Timothy Cole and the genetically mutated down at Cole's Comics.

Farewell and adieu.

CHAPTER ONE

It was a special Friday.

A Friday even more special than most Fridays were.

As the last day of the school week and the beginning of the weekend, Friday was always just plain awesome, but a Friday like this one took average, everyday Friday to new heights of awesomeness.

For this was a Friday before a long weekend.

There was no school on Monday, and that was a very cool thing. The only thing cooler was an unexpected day off before a weeklong break and, of course, summer vacation.

When the bell rang, bringing the school day to a close, Billy Hooten couldn't get to his locker fast enough. The gears were already turning inside his head and he only hoped three days off would be enough time.

Of course it is, he told himself, dialing the combination to his locker. *It's three whole days.*

The only possible crimp in his plans was Aunt Tilley. She was spending the weekend at Billy's house while her apartment at the Shady Acres Assisted Living Facility was being painted. He'd gone to visit her there a bunch of times over the years, but this was the first time she was coming to stay with him and his parents.

But Billy didn't think it would be too big of a deal. From what his mom and dad said, it sounded like old people pretty much slept all the time, and when they weren't sleeping, they just talked about the different kinds of medicine they were taking and what was wrong with them.

Billy thought that was all kind of weird, but he couldn't really see it interfering with his plans for the long weekend.

He grabbed his jacket, gave his schoolbooks a wave goodbye, and slammed the metal locker door shut until Tuesday morning.

" 'Joy, gentle friends,' " a voice cried out—a voice that could only have been Kathy B's.

Billy looked back down the hall to see his actress friend and his other buddies—Dwight, Danny and Reggie—coming toward him.

" 'Joy and fresh days of love accompany your hearts!' " Kathy B finished with a bow.

"Whatever you say," Billy said, hooking his nearly empty book bag over his shoulder.

Kathy B was always quoting from Shakespeare plays, and nobody ever knew what she was talking about. Maybe if she'd start quoting from classic television, like *Cap'n Danger: Stunt Monkey,* she'd have better luck.

"You're not even gonna try, are you?" Kathy B said, crossing her arms and giving Billy her *I'm so disappointed in you* stare.

"Sure, I'll try," Billy told her. "Just give me a few days. . . ." Then he caught the eyes of his pals. "Three whole days!" he shouted.

The four guys broke into cheers, jabbing their fists into the air as Kathy B looked on, shaking her head in disgust.

"I swear," she said. "You four become more like cavemen every day."

They laughed, giving high fives all around, and then, as if on cue, Randy Kulkowski skulked around the corner, his pet crony, Mitchell Spivey, at his side.

Billy's blood immediately froze in his veins. He could practically hear the thought process inside Randy's skull. It sounded like popcorn cooking in the microwave.

Randy suddenly raised his arms above his head.

3

"Three-day weekend!" he screamed. "Whooooo-hooooooo!"

Mitchell *whooooo-hooooooo*ed as well, and the two ran down the hallway as if someone were trying to steal their three days of freedom.

"That was close," Reggie said, nervously sucking wind through the most elaborate braces Billy had ever seen.

"For a minute there, I thought I might be spending my three days in the intensive care unit," Danny added.

"When my cousin the kung fu master teaches me some of his super kung fu, I won't let that guy get away with being such a jerk anymore," Dwight said. He squinted and threw his best tough-guy sneer in the direction Randy and Mitchell had gone in.

It was the first time Billy had heard about Dwight's kung fu–master cousin, but he doubted it would be the last.

They began walking down the hallway, headed for freedom.

"First thing I'm going to do when I get home is start that mummification project I've been thinking about," Danny said with a dreamy look in his eyes.

"What are you mummifying?" Billy asked, not sure he really wanted to know.

"I haven't got that far," Danny answered. "That's

one of the reasons I'm so darn happy about having the three days off. I'll have plenty of time to figure it out."

Billy glanced at Dwight and saw that he was practically jumping out of his skin to share his plans.

"I'm going to my cousin's for the whole weekend—" Dwight started.

"To learn super kung fu?" Billy interrupted.

Dwight looked as though he'd been slapped. "How did you know?"

"I'm writing a play about a young girl who brings peace to the world with her stunning beauty and love for the great bard Shakespeare," Kathy B said.

"Oh, science fiction. I like it," Reggie said, and then laughed so hard he began to choke.

"Look at him!" Kathy B screeched. "He's choking on his ignorance."

They all laughed then, even Kathy B, as Reggie finally got control of himself, wiping away the drool that had started to flow as a result of the elaborate wirework inside his mouth.

"If you survive your laughing fit, what're you doing this weekend, Reg?" Billy asked him.

They had reached the doors and pushed them open, exiting into the winter chill.

"I might just do nothing," the boy said with a nod. "Yeah, that sounds good. I'm gonna sit around and when my mother asks me what I'm doing, I'm gonna tell her, 'Absolutely nothing.' "

"Oh, that sounds like fun," Billy lied.

"Yeah, doesn't it?" Reggie said with a twisted glint in his eye.

Billy was sure that inside his friend's brain, Reggie was already doing nothing.

"All right, Hooten," Dwight said as he zipped up the cool jacket his father had brought him back from an Arctic research base or something like that. "What's going on with you this weekend?"

Billy knew that there would be Owlboy adventures in Monstros City—oh yes, there would—and that they would be far more exciting than anything his pals had going on, but he couldn't tell them anything about those, 'cause they'd think he was crazy.

Well, at least crazier.

"I'm gonna reread and organize all my comics, maybe do some drawing and stuff . . ." He paused, wondering if he needed to go on.

By the looks on his friends' faces, he could tell they weren't all that impressed.

"Oh yeah, and my great-aunt Tilley is coming for the weekend while they paint her apartment at the assisted living place."

"Your great-aunt Tilley?" Kathy B asked.

Billy nodded. "Yeah, she's my mom's aunt."

"She sounds old, Billy," Danny said. "Is she?"

Billy nodded again.

"You're gonna have an old person in your house for the whole weekend?" Reggie asked, his eyes nearly bugging from his crazy head.

"Yeah, what's wrong with that?"

They all started to laugh.

"Have you ever had an old person stay at your house before, Hooten?" Dwight asked, his tone of voice implying that he was speaking from experience, of course.

"No, but—"

"My grandmother lived with us for a while," Dwight said. "It was the worst thing ever. We could only have food that didn't have to be chewed. I've never had so much pudding in all my life."

"Old people are scary, Billy," Kathy B said. "There was this old guy who lived across the street from me and his skin was so thin I could see his veins pumping blood through him."

Reggie gasped, nearly choking on his saliva.

"I don't ever want to get old," he said, slowly shaking his head. "I hear that some of them actually take their teeth out at night and leave them in glasses on the sink."

Billy shuddered. Somehow his weekend didn't seem so promising after all.

Billy was in his closet, getting his Owlboy costume ready for the night's adventuring, when he heard the first thump.

Billy quickly shoved the costume into his book bag and dropped the bag on the floor just inside the door, ready to go.

He stepped out of the closet and slowly closed the door, listening for any more unusual sounds. He heard another thump, followed by his parents' voices coming from the room next to his—the junk room.

Every house had one. It was the room stuffed with junk no one knew what to do with but nobody could throw away. The Hootens' junk room had it all: old clothes, Christmas decorations, stereo equipment, VCRs, furniture, Billy's old baby toys and his school papers from kindergarten.

Billy opened the door to his room and peeked outside to find his parents moving things out of the junk room.

"What are you doing?" he asked, stepping into the hallway.

"Moving this stuff so your aunt Tilley will have a place to sleep," Billy's father replied, hefting a big green trash bag filled with who knew what and dropping it onto the floor in the hall.

"There's a bed in there?" Billy craned his neck to see over the stacks of stuff. "Really?"

"That's one of the things usually found in a guest room," his mother said. She had a large plastic Santa in her arms and it looked as if the two of them were about to dance.

She stopped, glancing back into the room. "At least, I think there's a bed in there. . . . There used to be one . . . I think."

"There's a bed in here," Dad said, rolling his eyes as he went back in.

"Why are you putting it all out here?" Billy asked, tempted to give them a hand. He was curious about what he might find if he dug down deep enough. He imagined himself lifting a box and discovering the fossil of some long-dead prehistoric beast. He smiled. . . .

But not for long.

"We're bringing it out here before we put it in your room," his father said, carrying out an old chair with ripped seat cushions.

"What!" Billy screeched.

"Don't get your Underoos in a knot," Dad said, dropping the chair. "It's only temporary. We'll move it all back out as soon as Aunt Tilley leaves on Monday."

"But . . . but . . ."

Billy was stunned. He couldn't imagine what it

would be like to have all this . . . this garbage inside his bubble of calm . . . his fortress of solitude. *It'll be more like the castle of crap with all this stuff crammed inside*, he thought. He wondered if there would even be enough room for oxygen.

"I protest!" he cried.

Mom and Dad, their arms loaded with odds and ends, stopped their work and stared at him.

Billy folded his arms and gave them one of his formidable glares. It had once stopped a Draconian Shriek Beetle dead in its tracks.

"Too bad," Dad said, dropping his armful and heading back into the spare room for some more.

So much for formidable glares, Billy thought, never having realized that his father could be made of sterner stuff than a Draconian Shriek Beetle.

"Sorry, hon," Mom said with a shrug. "There's just no other place to put this stuff. I promise we'll have it all moved out as soon as your great-aunt leaves."

"But . . . but I protested," Billy sputtered.

"Yeah, I guess you did. Good job," his mother said, turning to help his father carry out a stuffed giraffe wearing a pair of dark sunglasses and a red bandana around its long neck.

Like a prisoner on death row, Billy went into his room to await the inevitable. There would be no call from the governor to stop this atrocity. And before he

knew it, his parents had invaded his space, carrying in piece after piece, until his room started to take on a disturbing new appearance.

It looked like the junk room!

Not only did Billy's room look like Filthy Pete's Salvage Yard, but it took forever for the usual Friday-night Hooten tradition to begin.

Every Friday night, Dad would get takeout from the Chinese Dragon and pick up a movie from the Video Vault downtown. But since moving all the junk from the guest room to Billy's had taken so long, Dad started to complain about being too tired to get the takeout and the movie.

All it took was Mom's starting to talk about making her tuna-noodle surprise, and suddenly Billy's father had a burst of energy.

But everything was late: the food, the movie, the parents' falling asleep in front of the television—and Billy's sneaking out of the house to Monstros City for a little Owlboy action before bedtime.

He almost considered skipping the superhero antics for the night, but when he got another look at his room, he couldn't wait to get out of there.

His parents were out like lights, the work of emptying the guest room having sent them both into such a deep, snoring sleep that not even the giant asteroid rocketing through space on a collision course with Earth on TV could wake them from their slumber.

And that was fine by Billy.

He had some superheroing to do.

It was amazing how good he'd become at sneaking out of the house at night. With his backpack slung over his shoulder, Billy bolted out the back door and down the steps of his porch to the great stone wall that separated his backyard from the Pine Hill Cemetery. Within seconds he had made it over the wall and was running down the path that would take him to the Sprylock family mausoleum, the entrance to Monstros City.

As he changed into his costume in the musty burial chamber, he was already thinking about the kinds of adventures that might be in store for him that night. While rereading some of the back issues in his Owlboy comic collection, he'd recently come across a story about the Brain Eaters of Sygnis 5. He couldn't remember if he'd gone up against them yet. Maybe this would be the night!

In full Owlboy costume, Billy marched to the stone crypt at the back of the mausoleum. The heavy lid was slightly askew, and he slid it to the side to allow himself better access.

Billy eased himself down into the inky blackness as if he were sliding into a cool bath. Activating the special Owlvision lenses in his goggles, he descended the winding stone steps, down, down, down into another world.

The world of Monstros City.

He heard the clanging of alarms before he'd gotten even halfway down. Careful not to fall, Billy quickened his pace to the bottom and ran as fast as he could within the many passages of darkness that would take him to one of the back doors of the supersecret headquarters of Owlboy—the Roost.

"What's all the noise for?" Billy yelled over the ringing alarms as he entered a room filled with row upon row of old television sets stacked as high as the rounded ceiling. This was the monitoring room, where Owlboy and his team kept a close eye on the goings-on in the city of monsters.

A crazy-eyed goblin dressed in a tuxedo with tails came at him from around a corner, stubby arms waving frantically in the air.

"There's trouble at police headquarters. . . . There's not a second to lose!" Archebold, Owlboy's goblin sidekick, screeched, grabbing his arm and dragging him from the monitor room and down the hallway.

"What kind of trouble?" Billy asked, allowing himself to be pulled along.

"The big kind," Archebold said, pushing the button to open the elevator doors.

The two of them scrambled inside as soon as the doors slid open.

"It's not the Brain Eaters of Sygnis 5 by any chance, is it?" Billy asked as the elevator, and his stomach, dropped on their way to the garage level.

"We could only be so lucky," the goblin said, rushing out of the elevator toward the Owlmobile. The sleek yellow vehicle had been pulled out of its parking spot inside the garage and was waiting for them.

Halifax, a troll, as well as Monstros City's greatest mechanic and handyman, stood by the vehicle, hands shoved into the deep pockets of his grease-stained overalls.

"All gassed up and ready to go," the troll said as Archebold climbed behind the wheel.

"Thanks, buddy," the goblin said.

"Hey, Halifax," Billy said with a wave, climbing into the passenger seat. "Off to combat evil. Talk to you when I get back."

"Have fun," the troll responded, watching as they drove out of the garage and into action.

The Roost was hidden inside a gigantic tree—the biggest in all of Monstros City—that grew in the center of the Wailing Wood. The Owlmobile raced down a curvy road carved into the center of one of the tree's enormous branches to the road that would take them from the woods to the nighttime streets of Monstros.

It was always nighttime in Monstros City.

"So, what's the trouble?" Billy asked, psyching himself up for the adventure to come. "Vampires?"

"Nope," Archebold said, keeping his eyes on the road.

"Killer robots?"

"Nope."

"Flying monkeys?"

Archebold smiled as he took a sharp right and then a left, narrowly avoiding what looked like a tyrannosaur that had stopped in the middle of the street to tie its sneaker.

"Flying monkeys are cool . . . but no," the goblin said as they hit an area of town that Billy recognized as the neighborhood of the Monstros City Police Headquarters. "You're going to need to see this one to believe it."

Billy looked out the window, expecting to see the huge stone building that housed the Monstros City Police Department, but all he saw was an open space where he was sure the building was supposed to be.

"Hey, wait a minute," Billy said, momentarily confused. "Are you sure we're on the right street?"

"We're on the right street, all right," the goblin said, pulling over to a parking spot across from the open lot.

They both got out of the Owlmobile and crossed the street to join a growing crowd of Monstros citizens.

"This can't be right," Billy said, reaching the curb.

"Oh, it's right," Archebold said, then excused himself as he moved through the gathering to reach the open lot.

Billy followed close at the goblin's heels, feeling the excitement around him grow.

"It's him!"

"Owlboy will find a way to make this better."

"I thought he'd be taller."

"What did we do without him for so long?"

Billy smiled as he listened to their words about him—about *Owlboy*—and knew that he'd never get tired of hearing them.

Archebold stood on the sidewalk before the open section of land and pointed. "Look," the goblin said.

Billy wasn't exactly sure what he was supposed to be looking at, and even considered activating one of the many pieces of gadgetry built into his goggles to help him see better, but then he saw it.

At first he thought that somebody had simply left a toy in the lot, but as he looked more closely, he saw that the toy was an exact replica of police headquarters. It was about the size of one of his five-year-old next-door neighbor's dollhouses, but it had much more detail.

"Why would somebody make a toy of police headquarters?" Billy asked, looking to Archebold for answers.

The goblin shook his bumpy head. "It's not a toy."

The words started to sink in as Billy approached the tiny structure. "Not a toy?" he asked. "So you're saying that this little building is actually . . ."

Billy bent forward for a closer look, reaching into one of the pockets of his utility belt to remove his magnifying glass.

"You gotta be freakin' kidding me!" Billy exclaimed, looking through the thick lens at a tiny Chief Bloodwart waving up from the steps of the miniaturized police station.

"Told ya it would bake your noodle," Archebold said.

"What happened?" Billy asked, putting down the magnifying glass to observe the four inch-tall police officers staring up at him.

"We got the call as it was happening," Archebold said. "Don't have a clue as to who's responsible. In this burg you could put together a list a mile long of villains with a grudge against law enforcement."

Billy could see that Chief Bloodwart was trying to speak with him, but the policeman's usually rough, gravelly voice sounded like tiny mouse squeaks.

"I can't hear you," Billy said with a shake of his head.

The chief said something to one of his men, who ran inside the building. Within moments he returned with a teeny-tiny megaphone and handed it to the chief.

"Can you hear me now, Owlboy?" Bloodwart called up to Billy, his tiny voice amplified.

Billy gave him the thumbs-up.

"Any idea who could have done this to you?" Billy asked.

The chief and his officers shook their misshapen heads.

"No idea other than the fact that whoever is responsible is rotten to the core," Bloodwart growled into the megaphone. "To think that someone could do such a thing . . . it makes you lose faith in your fellow monsters."

"I hear ya," Archebold said in agreement.

Billy knew that they needed to do something to restore the Monstros City Police Department to its full size, and they needed to do it fast. And it was up to Owlboy to make it happen.

"Don't worry, Chief," Billy said. "We'll find the person responsible for this heinous act, and force them to return you to your normal size."

The tiny police officers started to cheer.

"Good luck, Owlboy!" Chief Bloodwart cried through the megaphone.

And without wasting any more time, Billy and Archebold were on the move.

Already working the case.

CHAPTER TWO

"They were so tiny and cute," Archebold said, and started to giggle. "I wanted to pick them all up and put them in my pockets."

He was driving the Owlmobile away from the miniaturized police station as Billy slowly turned to look at him.

"What?" he asked, not sure if he had heard correctly.

"The little policemen," Archebold answered. "They were so tiny and helpless that I just wanted to take them back to the Roost and put them in a nice, comfy cage and let them run on a wheel all day long."

"You're scaring me," Billy said. "That's Chief Blood-wart you're talking about . . . very rocky and very scary, most of the time."

"He was the cutest one of all," Archebold said with

another giggle and a shake of his head. "I've always wanted pets."

"You can't keep the Monstros City Police force as pets!" Billy yelled. "That's just nuts. We have to find out who did this to them and make whoever's responsible return them to their normal size."

"Imagine if you had a really bad itch," Archebold said as he drove. "Y'know, one of those real bad ones that you can't reach. You could just drop one of the little fellas down your shirt and have them go to town."

Billy just stared, not believing what he was hearing.

"Okay," he said slowly. "I didn't actually hear what you just said, and instead heard about how concerned you are with finding the villains responsible for shrinking Chief Bloodwart and his men."

"Sorry," Archebold said with a shrug. "It's just that—"

Billy held up a gloved hand. "We're done with that, thank you very much. Now, where's the *Book of Creeps?*"

"It's in the backseat," the goblin said, bringing the Owlmobile to a stop at a red light.

Billy reached over the seat to grab the ancient tome and placed it on his lap. "All right, let's see what we've got here," he said, licking the end of his finger and starting to flip the pages. "First we have to figure out how it was done."

"Wasn't magic," Archebold said with a shake of his squash-shaped head.

"How do you know?" Billy asked.

"Didn't smell like magic," the goblin said, his hands locked on the steering wheel. "Magic has a very distinct smell."

"What's it smell like?"

Archebold thought for a moment. "Like bananas mixed with gasoline," he said with a firm nod.

Billy wrinkled his nose. "Guess you're right, then, 'cause I didn't smell anything like that at the scene of the crime."

"Which really doesn't mean that magic wasn't used," Archebold added. "They could've used a magical spell to disguise the fact that magic was used."

Billy thought for a moment before drawing his own conclusions.

"Yeah, but if magic smells like bananas and gasoline, wouldn't that mean we'd just be smelling more bananas and gasoline if a special spell was used?"

"Not necessarily," Archebold said.

"Y'know what, this is giving me a headache," Billy said as he went back to the *Book of Creeps*. "For now we'll ignore the magical creeps and focus on the creeps with a background in mad science."

"Suit yourself," Archebold said. "You're the costumed hero."

Billy furiously flipped through the pages, reviewing the most dangerous geniuses in Monstros. Most of them had the scientific know-how to perform such a dastardly act, but most also were already locked away in Beelzebub Prison or had fallen victim to one of their insane scientific schemes.

Billy thought briefly of poor Dr. Evilus, who had accidentally transformed himself into a living wedge of cheese and was set upon by his hungry lab rats.

Poor devil. That was awful. Just awful.

"Well, I'm getting nothing here," Billy said, slamming the creepy book closed.

"Maybe if we question some of the Monstros criminal element . . . ," Archebold suggested.

"Hmmmm," Billy said, stroking his chin. "Y'know, that's a pretty good idea. I just bet whoever was responsible had to go and talk to some of his bad-guy buddies."

"They do like to talk," the goblin said with a nod.

"That means we have to take a drive to a bad part of town," Billy said.

"All part of the job, sir," Archebold said, making sure that the doors were locked.

"All right, then." Billy tossed the *Book of Creeps* into the backseat.

"Take us to where the bad guys like to hang out," he said. "Take us to Big Freddy's."

* * *

Big Freddy's was bad news with a capital B and N and with a couple of exclamation points thrown in at the end for good measure.

Anyone looking for trouble was sure to find it there. Big Freddy's was like a magnet for badness, plus they served burgers and drinks.

Billy had been there a few times already, when he'd needed to get the word out that Owlboy was back.

The Owlmobile turned down Desolation Lane, the lonely street where Freddy's was located. Of course there weren't any parking spaces, so Billy told Archebold to drop him off in front, then join him after he had found a space.

"Are you sure?" Archebold asked, double-parking beside what looked like a flying saucer. Yep, Big Freddy's even attracted them from out of state.

"I'll be fine," Billy said, opening his door. "By the time you find a spot and join me back here, I'll probably have the names of the guy who shrunk the police force and twenty other evildoers."

"Only twenty?" Archebold asked. "Must be a slow night."

Billy slammed his door, then watched for a moment as the yellow Owlmobile drove away and was swallowed by the darkness.

He checked out his reflection in the shiny

surface of the UFO, wanting to be sure that he looked all right.

Quite the striking figure, he thought, positive that if he were a villain, he'd be shaking in his boots. He walked toward the doors.

Big Freddy's didn't look like anything from the outside: it was just a plain old brick building, its two front windows covered with yellowed shades. To the unknowing, it would look abandoned, but to those in the know, it was a nest of evil.

Billy threw open the door and strode inside. They didn't notice him at first, most of them caught up in their evil conversations or drinking their evil drinks and eating their evil appetizers while evil music—*something by Michael Jackson*—played on the evil jukebox.

He looked around, trying to catch one of their eyes—some of these guys had up to twelve of them on their heads!—but still they didn't seem to notice, all of them busy with their evil socializing.

Not sure how to make a scene, Billy walked over to the bar, pushing himself between two Big Freddy's patrons, one who resembled a stalk of broccoli and another who looked like a heaping pile of spaghetti—only with lots of eyes.

He slammed his hand down onto the bar top to get the bartender's attention. The bartender was a giant beast, all fur and fangs, wearing an apron and drying a beer mug with a dirty rag.

"Gimme something fizzy," Billy said in his gruffest voice.

The mug fell from the monster's hand and smashed on the floor.

It was about time somebody noticed Billy.

"Owlboy," the monster bartender growled as the patrons on either side moved away.

"Huh," Billy said, enjoying the reaction. "So I finally have your attention."

The jukebox suddenly went quiet, along with the rest of the bar, as the news of their special visitor spread like a stomach virus in a first-grade classroom.

"What . . . what do you want?" the bartender asked nervously. The last time Billy had been in, he'd been pursuing the Gangrene Gang, who had knocked over a jewelry store and were attempting to use Big Freddy's as a place to hide from the police.

The police didn't find them, but Owlboy did.

There had been a bit of a scuffle, and Billy had been forced to use some of his special fighting skills to apprehend the criminals. Some tables and chairs had been damaged in the process.

"I'm looking for some information," Billy said now.

"We ain't got none of that here," the bartender

said. "Ain't that right, fellas?" he screamed to the crowd.

The gathering of beasts agreed, with a series of grunts, squeaks and roars.

Just then a door opened at the back of the establishment and Billy watched as a short monster, its body covered in sharp-looking quills like a porcupine's, came in and walked across the floor toward them. The porcupine beast was carrying a glass jar filled with a clear greenish fluid. In the fluid floated a bald head.

Billy felt honored. It wasn't often that one got to talk to Big Freddy.

The porcupine monster carefully set the glass jar down on the bar top and disappeared behind the counter. Big Freddy, his eyes magnified by the green fluid and the thickness of the jar, stared out at him.

The porcupine creature then returned with what looked like a black stereo speaker, and set it beside the glass jar. He took a wire from the back of the speaker and plugged it into the base of the jar.

The speaker screeched loudly with feedback; then Big Freddy's voice filled the room.

"Can you hear me all right, hero?" the head asked with a gurgle.

"I can hear you fine," Billy said. "How's it going, Freddy?"

"It was goin' great until you walked through the door," Freddy answered with a snarl.

"Sorry to ruin your night, but I need some information," Billy said.

"Hrrrumph," Big Freddy responded, green bubbles floating up from his mouth and nostrils. "That's very hard to come by these days," the disembodied head added. "It has to be earned before it is given."

"All right," Billy said. "How do I do that?"

The porcupine creature disappeared behind the bar again and reemerged with what appeared to be a box for some sort of game Billy had seen before.

Billy was ready for just about anything and expected the worst, but nothing could have prepared him for the reality.

" 'Twister'?" he read.

"Twister," Big Freddy gurgled in reply. "You have to play and beat one of our best."

Billy was shocked. Who would ever have expected that Twister would find its way to the world of monsters? Then again, it *was* a classic.

"You're on," Billy agreed, and a collective gasp went through the barroom.

The inside of the building came alive, the monstrous customers moving tables aside while others reverently laid the plastic mat with the multicolored dots down on the floor.

Billy knew the rules, having played the game one Christmas Eve at his uncle Michael's house. He still remembered the sound of Uncle Michael's back cracking and the moans of agony that followed. Their little game had put Uncle Michael in the hospital for three days.

Billy kicked off his rubber boots and approached the plastic game pad in his stocking feet. "Let's do this," he said, waiting to see who—*or what*—his opponent would be.

A murmur went through the crowd as they parted to let one of their own pass.

A skeleton wearing a bowler hat stepped forward and Billy gasped. He thought he knew this skinless creature. In fact, he had known three of them. He had encountered three skeleton criminals on his first visit to Monstros when they had been trying to rob a grocery store.

Fibula, Patella and Tibia, Billy thought as the skeleton stepped onto the Twister mat. He wondered which one this was.

"So, you're the Owlboy," the skeleton said. "Not as impressive as I was led to believe."

"You have me at a disadvantage," Billy said. "Who, might I ask, will I be facing off against in this game of dexterity and skill?"

"Femur," the skeleton said. "Femur of the Bony brothers."

"Ah yes," Billy said with a nod. "And how are your brothers?"

"Doing time in Beelzebub Prison, no thanks to you," the skeleton said. "And I'd be doing the same if I hadn't been . . . busy."

Another walking skeleton, this one wearing a blond wig and a slinky red dress, poked her head out from the crowd, the gold bracelets on her bony white arms jangling as she excitedly waved.

"Win this one for me, sweetie pie," she cried.

"I see," Billy said with a nod.

"I'm gonna win this one for my brothers," Femur said.

"You're certainly welcome to try," Billy answered, standing on one side of the dotted game pad, the skeleton on the other.

The speaker from the bar top whined noisily again as Big Freddy got set to start the game.

"Are we ready?" the floating head gargled.

Both Billy and Femur nodded, anticipating the game's beginning.

"Because we believe in fair play here," Freddy began, "we're going to allow Owlboy—since he is a visitor to our establishment—to have the first move."

Femur didn't have any problem with that. He removed his bowler hat and bowed to his opponent. "First or last—it doesn't matter," the skeleton said. "You're going to lose this one."

The porcupine creature held the spinner pad up to the glass jar so that Freddy could see, and gave its black arm a flick. The spinner spun and finally landed on Billy's first direction.

"Right foot red," Freddy announced, and Billy did what he was told, placing his stocking-covered right foot in the center of a red circle.

It was Femur's turn now.

The porcupine creature flicked the spinner.

"Left hand green," Freddy said, and the skeleton responded.

It went like that for what felt to Billy like days: rights and lefts, feet and hands, the two opponents intertwined like a couple of anacondas out on a date.

Billy had just moved his left hand to a yellow dot. Femur was draped over him, the skeleton's bare ribs poking Billy in the back. It was the Bony brother's turn, and Billy wasn't sure how much more of this he could take. His legs and arms were trembling with strain, and he knew that it was certainly possible that he could lose his balance at any second, though the same could be said about Femur.

The tension inside the barroom was as thick as

Jello-O, every monster in the joint hoping that Billy would fall to the mat. But he held on, even though his arms and legs were screaming like the girls in his first-grade class when he'd brought his presidential scab collection to school for show-and-tell, every scab shaped like one of the nation's great leaders. The Abraham Lincoln was particularly spectacular.

He had an awesome collection.

"Right foot red," Freddy gurgled, reading the spinner held before the glass jar by the porcupine beast.

Femur carefully brought his leg up and around in a move that only a skeleton—somebody minus flesh, muscle, veins and guts—could make.

And Billy knew then that there was a good chance he wasn't going to make it.

But the good fairy of Twister—or at least a little goblin—must have been in the neighborhood.

"What the heck is going on in here?" Archebold squawked, coming into Big Freddy's. He was eating what looked like some sort of fried animal on a stick, his face shiny with grease.

The sudden appearance of the goblin was all it took.

Femur shifted slightly to the right, the heel of his bony foot sliding out, and that was all she wrote. The skeleton tumbled down, his entire body breaking into pieces, as if somebody had hit a self-destruct button.

The bar patrons moaned in unison.

Before he himself could fall, Billy pulled out of his pretzel position and sprang to his feet.

"Where've you been?" he asked Archebold.

The goblin took a bite of his fried rodent. "Took me forever to find a space, and when I did, I saw this cart selling fried varmint and couldn't resist. Bite?" he asked, holding the greasy golden brown animal out for Billy.

"No, thanks," Billy said. "I'm gonna try for that information now."

"Awesome," Archebold said. "Good thing I got here when I did."

Billy walked across the mat toward Big Freddy, Femur's skull screaming as he passed.

"Not fair," Femur complained. "I got distracted."

"Better luck next time," Billy said. "But now I'm going to collect my prize."

They'd started to return the bar to normal, pushing the tables and chairs back, rolling up the Twister mat, sweeping Femur's parts into a big pile so that his girlfriend with the many bracelets could put him back together.

"You won fair and square, Owlboy," Big Freddy said from inside his glass jar. "So what can I do for you?"

The bar went quiet, all the patrons suddenly listening for the reason he had come. Probably listening just in case they wanted to make a run for the door if it was them he was looking for.

"The police station and everybody inside got shrunk, and I want a handle on who's responsible so that I can bring them in and get Monstros City law enforcement back to normal size."

"Oh, is that all?" Big Freddy asked. "That's an easy one."

Billy suddenly noticed that everybody in the bar was looking in one direction, and that everybody was quiet except for a single voice.

"I shrunk them down," said the voice, followed by a crazy giggle. "Yes, I did, I shrunk 'em down to the size of insects. Let's see 'em arrest me now. Not so tough, are they? I think I could use another drinky."

There was more insane laughter, and Billy and Archebold moved toward it.

A lone figure, surrounded by empty glasses of what looked like joy juice, was sitting at a tiny table. The man seemed normal enough, except that his skin was awfully baggy, hanging from his body as if it were three sizes too big.

"Oh jeez," Archebold said between bites of his varmint on a stick. "Figures it's him."

" 'Him' who?" Billy asked, watching as the man swayed drunkenly in his seat, talking to nobody in particular.

Archebold walked over to the man and gave him a poke.

"Hey, you!" the goblin said, and the man with the loose-fitting skin spun around in his chair.

"Yes?" he asked, obviously trying to keep his vision focused.

"You're Dr. Bug, right?" Archebold asked him.

"Why, yes," Dr. Bug responded. "How nice to be noticed."

"Why's his skin so loose?" Billy asked the goblin.

The doctor overheard the question, standing up from his seat on spindly legs. "It's because I'm wearing a disguise, dear lad," the man whispered so loudly that everybody inside Big Freddy's could hear.

He then tugged at the skin around his mouth and pulled it up and over himself to reveal the head of a really large and gross-looking insect.

It looked like a cockroach to Billy.

"Behold the true face of the genius that is Dr. Bug!" the villain proclaimed.

"Did you shrink the Monstros City Police Department?" Billy asked him.

"I certainly did," Dr. Bug answered proudly. "I used my latest invention." He reached into his pocket, pulled out a crazy-looking gun and began to wave it around.

"It is my shrink gun," he said. "With it I can reduce

37

anyone or anything to the size of the tiniest germ if I so please."

Billy stepped forward and snatched the shrink gun from his hand. "I'll take that," he said. "Before you shrink anybody else."

"Hey," Dr. Bug protested. "That's mine!"

"Not if you're going to use it for evil," Billy said.

Archebold finished up his fried varmint and tossed the empty stick onto Dr. Bug's table. Then he and Billy each took one of Dr. Bug's arms, marching the evil scientific genius toward the door.

"But that's what I'm all about," the insect wearing the man suit proclaimed. "I'm all about being bad!"

"And that's why you're in the situation you're in right now," Billy told him as they ushered the man out the door.

"Thanks for the game!" Billy cried, giving Big Freddy and the monstrous patrons a final wave as they headed out of the bar.

The ride back to the police station couldn't have been over soon enough.

In the back of the Owlmobile, the villainous Dr. Bug had started to cry, carrying on about how he never got any respect from the supervillain community and how he had been hoping that his break would come with the invention of his shrink gun and the shrinking of the Monstros police force.

Billy started to feel sort of bad for the guy but reminded himself that this was a villain who had done a pretty nasty thing.

"Don't give us a hard time about restoring the police department and its headquarters, and we'll mention that you helped us out to the folks over at Beelzebub Prison," Billy suggested to the crying insect.

"Maybe they'll go easy on you," Archebold added, pulling the Owlmobile over to the curb and the crowd that was still hanging around the space where the police station had stood. "Let you keep your human suit, maybe."

"Do you think?" Dr. Bug asked hopefully.

"Anything's possible," Billy said, climbing out of the car and tipping the passenger seat forward so that the doctor could climb out.

"I love my human suit," the doctor said. "Without it I feel so naked."

Billy and Archebold escorted the insect through the crowd, toward where the miniature police station still stood.

"Recognize this?" Archebold asked the villain.

"Oh yes," Dr. Bug answered, his pincers clicking together. "I'm so very proud. It's my finest work." He started to sniffle.

"All right, enough with the waterworks," Billy told

him gruffly. Dr. Bug had to be the weepiest villain he'd ever encountered. Really, it was no wonder he didn't get any respect from the other bad guys.

"Is this the perpetrator?" Chief Bloodwart squawked from the tiny megaphone.

"It certainly is, Chief," Billy replied. "And he said that he'd help us out by returning you to normal if we put a good word in for him with the warden over at Beelzebub."

"The thought of doing anything nice for someone like this—" Bloodwart began.

"He wants to keep his human suit," Archebold interrupted.

"Oh," the chief answered.

"So you think we could make a deal?" Billy asked him.

"Yeah, it's possible," the chief answered grudgingly. "But he better do something right this minute, because I'm getting pretty tired of this nonsense."

Billy pulled the shrink gun from where he'd hung it on his utility belt. "Did you hear that, Dr. Bug?" Billy asked him. "No funny business. Reverse what you've done and the chief will put in a good word for you."

"I don't deserve this," the doctor said with a shake of his head; tears burst from his buggy compound eyes.

"Oh brother," Archebold said, rolling his own eyes.

Billy shoved the gun into Bug's hand, the baggy skin looking like a loose rubber glove. "Take this and do your thing."

"I want to thank you for this opportunity," Dr. Bug began, wiping tears away.

"Just do it," Billy said, giving his arm a push.

The doctor studied the gun for a moment, reaching down with saggy fingers to adjust a series of buttons on the side of the weapon. "That should do it," he muttered to himself before pointing the shrink gun down at the police headquarters and the miniaturized officers that scurried around it.

The gun started to hum as he pulled the trigger, and a twisting, turning beam of colored light fired from the weapon and enveloped the police station in a bubble of crackling energy.

Billy tensed, but the villain had been true to his word, and Billy watched in awe as the station and the police officers began to grow.

They had to jump back as the station squeezed to fit between the two buildings on either side.

The rock-bodied Chief Bloodwart stood on the steps of the restored building, he himself restored to his full, ominous form.

Dr. Bug lowered the weapon. "There, it's done." He looked toward Billy.

Billy took the shrink gun from the villain. "I'll take that back, thank you," he said.

He handed it to Chief Bloodwart.

"You might want to put this somewhere safe," Billy told him. "Wouldn't want it falling into the wrong hands."

"Right you are, Owlboy," the chief said. He then handed it off to an officer who resembled a large salamander. "Put this in evidence storage," he told the amphibian.

Bloodwart turned his icy stare to Dr. Bug.

"And you," he growled, motioning for more of his officers to approach. "We've got a nice cell waiting for you before you begin your journey to Beelzebub Prison."

An officer grabbed hold of the doctor, slapping handcuffs around the loose-fitting skin of his wrist.

"Would it help if I said I was sorry?" he asked as they dragged him away, his human mask flapping at the back of his neck like a hood.

Billy, Archebold and the chief watched as he was taken inside police headquarters.

"I owe you a great debt of gratitude, Owlboy," Chief Bloodwart said, reaching down to shake Billy's hand.

"Don't mention it, Chief," Billy said, his hand lost within the rocky grip of the police chief. "It's all part of the job."

And with those words, Billy looked at his goblin companion.

"Come, Archebold," he said. "I'm sure there are other wrongs afoot that need our attention."

The two dashed to the waiting Owlmobile amid the clapping of the citizens gathered outside.

"I'm beat." Billy slumped in the passenger seat, removing his helmet and goggles.

"We'll rest up a bit and then get in touch with Halifax back at the Roost to see if anything is up," Archebold said, steering the car down one of the dark Monstros City streets.

"I'm wicked tired," Billy said. "I think I might call it a night."

Archebold looked at him. "Really? But we're just getting started."

"I know," Billy agreed. "And I'd really like to stay and smash some more evil, but I've got a real busy day tomorrow and I think I might need a good night's sleep."

The goblin seemed disappointed but was quick to accept Billy's decision.

"I guess the evil can wait," he said. "Give it a chance to become even more evil. So, what's going on tomorrow?"

"I'm going with my parents to pick up my great-aunt Tilley," Billy explained, watching the city of monsters whip past the passenger-side window. "Her apartment is being painted and she's going to be staying with us a few days until it's done."

"Great-aunt Tilley," Archebold said with a nod. "Is she old?"

"Yeah," Billy answered.

"Ever live with an old person before . . . even for a few days?"

"Why?" Billy asked, dreading what the goblin might add.

"Oh, nothing," Archebold said with a shake of his head. "I'm sure it'll be perfectly fine."

The inside of the Owlmobile then got very quiet. Billy was starting to question what exactly he was getting himself into that weekend; the more he thought about it, the more horrible it sounded.

CHAPTER THREE

The two monsters watched as the Owlmobile drove off.

Then they looked away from the brightly colored car and back at the fully restored police station. Both of them sneered, trudging off into the night.

"I thought he'd really done it this time, Mukus," the thinner of the two monsters, with skin the color of a bloodstain, stated. "I've always been a fan of Dr. Butt."

"It's Bug," Mukus, the plumper and drippier of the two, said, correcting him. "Dr. Bug. Why can't you get anybody's name right, Klot?"

"Are you sure?" Klot asked, bringing a long clawed finger up to his pointed chin. "I've been calling him Dr. Butt for years. It's no wonder he's never liked me."

"Ya think?" Mukus asked with a roll of his bulbous eyes.

The two trudged down the darkened Monstros street. At a Monstros City subway system entrance that was closed for repair work, they looked around to be certain that nobody was watching. Then they ducked beneath the chain that had been placed across the stairway, descending the litter-strewn steps into an even deeper darkness.

"So, who's going to tell him?" Klot asked nervously, breaking the silence of the deserted subway station.

"I told him the last time," Mukus said, walking toward the edge of the station platform. A ladder was there, and he started the climb down onto the tracks.

"Are you sure?" Klot asked, following his round friend down the ladder.

"Don't you remember?" Mukus said. "I told him about how Owlboy had stopped the Sludge Sloggers . . . ruining his burglary operations."

"Oh yeah," Klot said. "He was real mad about that one, but I think he was even madder when I told him about how the Bounder Boys had already been caught and sent back to Beelzebub, and how they'd only been out of jail less than a week."

"Doesn't matter. I gave the last bit of bad news, so it's your turn."

Klot's shoulders slumped as he and his friend continued down the subway tunnel. "Sometimes it just doesn't pay to be the lackeys for Monstros City's criminal mastermind," he said.

"You don't have to tell me," Mukus agreed. "Since Owlboy's come back to the city, it's been nothing but stress. I've got stomach pain all the time."

The plump monster belched loudly, the disgusting sound echoing down the dark tunnel.

"See?" he said.

"We were doing so good before *he* had to come back and spoil everything," Klot moaned. "That's the problem with these do-gooders: always raining on our parade."

Mukus looked at his friend. "Raining on our parade?" he repeated, not sure if he'd heard his friend right.

"What, not a good analogy?" Klot asked.

"Let's just agree that he's ruined everything and leave it at that," Mukus said angrily, his short stubby legs propelling him down the subway tunnel.

A giant mechanical rat pounced from the shadows into their path.

"YEEEEEEEEEEEEK!" Mukus squealed, falling backward into his friend's arms.

"Who goes there?" asked a voice from a speaker located within the mechanical rodent's mouth.

"It's us, great Monarch," Klot said. "Your faithful lackeys, Klot and Mukus."

"Oh, you," the voice from the speaker responded disappointedly. "I was hoping for a trespasser that I could terrify."

"No need to be disappointed, sir," Mukus said, removing himself from Klot's arms. "You did just fine."

The large robot rat turned around and darted off down the tunnel, its segmented metal tail dragging behind it.

"Proceed to my domicile," the Monarch of Crime ordered. "I hope you are bringing me good news of tonight's endeavors . . . for your sakes."

The monsters looked at each other and gulped.

Grudgingly, the two followed the mechanical rat down a tunnel obstructed with multiple barriers, and eventually arrived at an unfinished subway station.

The pair nervously climbed up onto the platform. The giant clockwork rat sat obediently beside the red-robed form of the Monarch. A black-gloved hand reached out from beneath the scarlet robes.

"That's a good girl," the Monarch purred affectionately, his face hidden in the shadows created by the deep hood that covered his head, as he scratched behind one of the ears of the large metal beast.

"I think she likes you," Klot said. He reached his red spidery hand out to pat the mechanical animal.

The robot rat lunged and snapped at his fingers, like a triggered bear trap.

The monster quickly pulled his hand back before he lost it.

"Of course she likes me," the Monarch said. "I made her. She is but one of the many inventions that have been spawned by my genius."

"You're a smart one; I've always said that about you," Mukus said with a smile. The fat monster was sweating profusely now, forming a sticky puddle on the ground at his chubby feet. "Didn't I always say that, Klot?"

"I really don't remember you ever saying much of anything about—" Klot began, but was halted by a fat hand placed over his mouth.

Mukus laughed nervously. "Always joking around," he said. "That's why I love him like a brother." He punched Klot in the stomach, and the thin red-skinned monster doubled over with a pained grunt.

But the Monarch didn't seem to be paying attention, continuing with the rant about his brilliance.

"A genius that has been used to aid the criminal element in their pursuit of power, a genius that will soon enable me to control the city of Monstros as its ruler . . . as its monarch."

Mukus started to clap enthusiastically. "Right you are. Long live the Monarch; that's what I say."

The crimson-robed criminal mastermind bowed to

the applause. "Thank you, thank you. Your loving adoration is greatly appreciated, and expected."

Klot gradually straightened himself out, rubbing his belly and joining in with a bit of clapping.

"So, what news do you bring me of tonight's forays into criminal activity?" the Monarch asked point-blank.

"I think that's something that Mukus would like to share with you," Klot suddenly blurted, stepping back and away from Mukus' chubby and dangerous hands.

"Very good," said the Monarch. He pushed a button on a section of nearby wall and a throne carved from a shiny black stone slid out from a hidden compartment. "Regale me with news of the nefarious wrongdoings of the criminal element," the crime boss said as he sat down upon his throne.

"Uhhh," Mukus began, not sure how to proceed.

"Go ahead, Mukus," Klot urged from a safe distance. "Regale him."

"Okay . . . sure . . . ahhhhhhhh, Dr. Bug, you remember him, right?" Mukus asked.

"Of course," the Monarch answered. "I helped him to perfect his shrink gun."

"Well, Dr. Bug shrunk the Monstros City Police Headquarters and everybody inside down to the size of dung beetles."

"You don't say," the Monarch replied excitedly.

"Yep," Mukus answered. "They were all screaming and carrying on. It was truly a victory for supervillainy everywhere."

"Brilliant!" the Monarch proclaimed, standing up from his throne to shake his black-gloved fists at the heavens. "Another victory for evil!"

"Yes, yes, it was," Mukus said. "And why don't you tell the Monarch what happened next, Klot?"

Klot gasped.

"Yes, faithful Klot," said the Monarch. "Enthrall me with villainy's next triumph. How did the insidious Dr. Bug proceed?"

Klot's brain tried to come up with something—anything but the truth. He had nothing.

"He was captured by Owlboy," the monster said, closing his eyes.

For a moment the Monarch said nothing, his eyes burning within the darkness of his cloak.

"What did you say?" the crime lord finally asked.

"Owlboy," Klot said, eyes still tightly closed. "Owlboy caught him at Big Freddy's and made him return everything to the right size and then he . . . Dr. Butt . . . Bug . . . he got arrested."

Klot kept his eyes shut, waiting for something bad to happen. The monster waited and waited, but nothing happened. Slowly, he cracked one bloodshot eye.

Mukus was standing perfectly still beside him. He appeared to be waiting for something as well.

The Monarch just stood in front of his stone throne, taking a series of deep breaths.

"He handled that much better than I expected," Klot whispered, nudging Mukus. And Mukus was turning toward him to agree just as the Monarch let out a bloodcurdling, mind-bending scream.

There was no doubt about it.

The Monarch was angry.

Despite the facts that he was exhausted and that it was now the Saturday of a long weekend, Billy couldn't sleep late no matter how hard he tried.

His eyes had opened bright and early, and he had just about had a heart attack, having forgotten about all the garbage that was now being stored in his room.

After he'd calmed himself down, he had decided to take it easy, reaching over to his desk for the comics he'd bought earlier in the week at the Hero's Hovel.

"C'mere, my pretties," he said with a grin, feeling that old excitement he always felt when he was about to read a comic. There wasn't a better feeling, and for the next hour or so, he lost himself in the fantastic world of heroes and villains.

And when he was done, returning to the normal world of his overly crowded bedroom, Billy decided that he wouldn't add to the clutter, and made the choice to file the new comics with his collection.

This was a precise procedure. First he had to bag the comic, sliding it carefully into the protective plastic sleeve. This was followed by the insertion of a backing board—a piece of cardboard specifically cut to the size of the plastic bag, to help keep the prized item from getting bent or damaged. And when that was done, the comic had to be filed—in alphabetical order, of course—in the special comic book boxes on the floor of his closet.

To Billy's disgust, he found that the comics inside the boxes felt very dusty. He couldn't stand for that. He grabbed an old T-shirt from his drawer and dusted them.

It was a dirty job, but somebody had to do it.

"Billy!" his mother called up from the foot of the stairs.

He leaped up from the floor, navigating some boxes, an old rocking chair, an umbrella stand and a trash bag filled with stuffed animals.

"Yeah?" he called back from the hallway outside his room.

"You better get dressed," his mother said. "We want to be out of here in ten minutes to pick up Aunt Tilley; we don't want to keep her waiting."

This is it, he thought as he put his comics away and got himself dressed. When Aunt Tilley had first been mentioned, he really hadn't given it much thought. He loved Aunt Tilley, but from what the gang at school had told him, and even Archebold's hinting, he gathered that there were some things he didn't know about old people.

He made his way downstairs, ate some frozen waffles and was ready to go.

He was pulling the back door of the Toyota open, about to get in, when he heard the familiar sound of plastic tires on the driveway and turned around to see his neighbor Victoria sitting astride her Princess Big Wheel.

"Good morning, Victoria," his mom said from the front seat as she fastened her seat belt.

"Where ya goin', Billy?" the five-year-old asked him.

"I'm going to pick up my aunt," he told the little girl. "She's gonna be staying with us for the weekend."

"Oh," she said, but he could practically see the gears turning inside the little kid's head. "Gonna be a superhero later?" she asked.

He gave her the evil eye. Owlboy and Monstros City were supposed to be a secret between them since the two had shared an adventure in the creepy city around Halloween.

"Nope, no superhero here," he said with a nervous laugh. "I'm too busy just being a kid." Billy climbed into the car. "You take care, now."

"How about tomorrow?" she asked. "Gonna be a superhero tomorrow?"

Billy slammed the car door, shaking a fist at the little girl and again giving her the hairy eyeball. He was going to have to have a long talk with the kindergartener about things she should and shouldn't talk about around adults.

She smiled, shaking her own tiny fist at him as the car backed down the driveway into the street.

But that talk with Victoria would have to wait; there was business to attend to now.

Business at a place called Shady Acres.

It looked like a pretty nice place from outside.

Aunt Tilley had moved to Shady Acres after her husband—Billy's great-uncle Fred—had died. They'd had their own house in Torrington, Massachusetts, which Billy and his folks had visited a few times over the years, but since Uncle Fred wasn't around anymore to help her take care of it, she had decided to move here.

Shady Acres was called an assisted living facility.

Billy wasn't sure exactly what that meant, but it looked like lots of old people lived there and somebody was there to take care of them if they needed help.

Not a bad idea, really, he thought as he walked with his folks into the nice brick building. It was warm, toasty, inside Shady Acres.

He remembered how worried his mom had seemed after Uncle Fred had died, afraid that something bad was going to happen to Aunt Tilley if she was alone. But now that she was at Shady Acres, nobody needed to worry anymore.

A nice lady in glasses with really thick lenses that made her eyes look wicked big was sitting at a desk in the small lobby. Mom told her why they were there, and the woman called up to Aunt Tilley's apartment to let her know that they were on their way up.

Billy noticed that there were old people everywhere: some reading newspapers, others sitting around the lobby talking, some on their way out. Billy didn't see anything all that scary about them. They didn't seem much different from anybody else—just wrinklier.

They rode up in the elevator with an old lady named Gert. They learned that she used to work for the post office, had two husbands, four children and ten grand-children and believed that there was nothing better than a nice piece of fish.

She got off on the third floor.

Just think of how much more we would have learned if she'd lived on the tenth floor like Aunt Tilley, Billy thought.

They reached the tenth floor and Billy ran ahead and knocked on Aunt Tilley's door with the knuckles of both hands. It took a moment, but the old woman finally opened the door with a huge smile and reached out to pull him close in a hug.

"Hey, Aunt Tilley," he said, his face pressed to her sweater.

There were hugs and kisses all around for him and his folks as Aunt Tilley invited them in. She'd already put a pot on for some tea, and while the water boiled, she showed them around her apartment.

Billy didn't think it was bad, though he did feel that the walls could use a new coat of paint. The color was a gross, pale pink that reminded him of the color of an Eluvian Sky Pig that he and Archebold had had to deal with a few weeks back when they had confronted Hezikiah the Demon Farmer and his Barnyard of Horrors.

The teakettle whistled and Aunt Tilley went to prepare their refreshment while Billy prepared to be bored.

"You should have brought some of your comic books," Dad said with a glance in his direction. "Probably gonna be a while."

"They got one of those big-screen television sets for the recreation room," Aunt Tilley suddenly said. "Fifty inches, I think it is."

"How nice," his mother answered. "I bet Billy would like one of those."

"Heck, I'd like one," Dad said.

Billy nodded. A television that big certainly would be awesome. He imagined how real the space battles from some of his favorite science fiction movies would look on a screen that size.

Awesome.

"Would you like to see it?" Aunt Tilley asked as she poured cups of tea from a fancy teapot. "The recreation room is on the seventh floor at the end of the hall. Go have a look if you like."

He decided that he'd really like to have a look, remembering that a *Transmogrifier* marathon had started that morning at nine—the first four seasons of the giant-robot show.

Giant robots on a fifty-inch television screen— could it get any better than that?

Billy looked to his father.

"Go ahead," his dad said. "We're gonna have tea and then hit the road." He looked at his watch. "You got twenty minutes."

Billy bolted for the door.

The elevator came and he got in, pushing the but-

58

ton for the seventh floor. He doubted that the old folks at Shady Acres would be watching the *Transmogrifier* marathon, but then again, one never knew.

The doors slid open and Billy stepped out, looking around to get his bearings. There were old people standing around talking; some were sitting in nice, comfy-looking chairs, reading newspapers and magazines.

He approached a group of four old people: there were three women with fancy-looking hair and one man who didn't have any hair. They seemed to be getting ready to go someplace.

"Excuse me," he said, to get their attention.

They looked his way and smiled.

"And who are you?" one of the women asked. Her hair was the craziest; it seemed to change from blue to silver, depending on the angle he looked at it.

"I'm Billy Hooten," he told her. "I'm here to pick up my aunt Tilley."

They all nodded.

"Tilley never mentioned she had such a handsome nephew," another of the women said with a wink. This one's hair was pure white. It looked like a soft-serve ice cream sitting on top of her head.

"When I was your age, I had five girlfriends," the old man said. "They loved my blond, wavy hair." He rubbed his bald head and looked disappointed. "Now I don't have any."

"That's too bad," Billy said. "I hear that there's a new fifty-inch television up here someplace. Do you know where?"

The old man pointed toward a doorway on the other side of the room. "It's in there and it's a real beauty," he said. "But I don't think you want to go in there now."

The old women looked at each other nervously.

"Yes, maybe it would be best if you came back later to see it," Blue Hair said . . . or was it silver?

"Is there something wrong with it?" Billy asked, staring at the doorway.

"No, nothing's wrong with the television; it's just that *he's* in there," the old man said.

"Who's 'he'?" Billy asked.

"Somebody who isn't at all pleasant," Soft Serve said, and, like a magician, pulled a Kleenex from within her sleeve and wiped her nose. "You're better off just not dealing with him."

Billy couldn't take his eyes off the entryway into the television room.

"But I really want to see the TV," he said.

"Suit yourself," the old man said. "We're not going to stop you."

Billy started to move toward the room.

"Very nice meeting you, Billy," Silver Hair said . . . or was it blue?

They all waved goodbye, and he returned the gesture as he headed into the television room. His eyes immediately went to the fifty-inch wide-screen television set mounted on the wall.

"Wow," he whispered to himself. The television was amazing, except that it was playing golf.

He looked around the TV room and saw that there was indeed somebody in there: a man sitting in a far, dark corner, arms folded across his chest, head slumped, fast asleep.

Billy could hear his deep, heavy breathing.

"Excuse me," Billy called gently.

The man didn't budge.

"I was wondering if you'd mind if I changed this," Billy said.

The man continued to sleep.

"What's that?" Billy then asked. "You say you don't mind at all? Why, thank you."

Billy looked for the remote and found it surrounded by magazines on a small coffee table. He'd had no idea there was a magazine called *Dentures Monthly*.

He picked the remote up and studied the buttons. It didn't seem all that different from the remote for the TV at home, other than the fact that this remote controlled a fifty-inch wide-screen plasma.

He pointed the remote at the television, punching

in the numbers of the channel he believed his beloved Transmogrifiers were playing on.

And suddenly, there they were in all their mechanical glory.

"Oh my gosh," Billy said, staring at the screen as two robots that had once been simple kitchen appliances did battle before his eyes.

This was one of his favorite episodes, and how lucky was he? This was his favorite part.

He thought he'd died and gone to heaven. . . .

Except for the old man's screaming.

"What the heck is going on!"

Billy turned to see the old man awake and on his feet. He was tall and skinny, his head almost bald but with wisps of white hair that floated in the air like some undersea plant life that Billy had seen once on Animal Planet.

"Who do you think you are, coming in here and changing the channel? Can't you see that I was watching that?"

Billy froze, watching in horror as the old man shuffled toward him on spindly legs.

"How were you raised, boy? By wolves, I'd guess, 'cause only a wolf would turn off a man's program while he was watching it."

The old man was right in front of him.

"So is that the case?" he demanded. *"Were you raised by wolves?"*

Billy said nothing, holding out the remote control to him. He tried to say that he was sorry, but the words wouldn't come.

He was *that* scared.

"Gimme that," the old man said, snatching the remote from his hand.

And as he fumbled with the buttons, grumbling angrily beneath his breath, Billy bolted for the door.

Now he understood what his friends had been telling him.

Old people *were* scary.

He couldn't stop thinking about it.

Here was Owlboy—*the Owlboy*, who had faced the vilest and most monstrous of villains—being chased from the television room of Shady Acres by a cranky old man.

"So, what did you think of the big TV?" Aunt Tilley asked, sitting beside him in the backseat of his parents' car.

He wanted to tell them all about his run-in with Cranky Old Man, but he was too embarrassed to bring it up.

"It was big," he said, looking out the window and watching traffic go by.

Aunt Tilley laughed. "It certainly is. I thought they'd put in a new window when I first saw it."

His parents laughed in the front seat, but he didn't see anything funny at the moment. The old man had really scared him, and now he felt completely embarrassed.

He wasn't sure how he would ever be able to put on the Owlboy costume again if Archebold and Halifax found out about this.

He suddenly imagined all the residents of Shady Acres standing outside the television room, desperate to watch TV, but Cranky Old Man was preventing them from entering. Then Billy was there, in his superhero costume, charging into the room. It was up to him—to *Owlboy*—to liberate the room.

Cranky Old Man wielded the remote as if it were some kind of cosmic weapon, trying to destroy him with bolts of crackling blue energy, but Owlboy was too fast. He snatched away the remote and turned it against its user. All that remained of Cranky Old Man after the furious battle was a pair of dentures lying in the middle of the television room floor.

And then the room was filled with cheers as the residents of Shady Acres raised their canes and walkers in salute to their hero. . . .

"Owlboy! Owlboy! Owlboy! Owlboy!"

As the Toyota pulled into the driveway of his house, Billy couldn't wait to get inside, grab his book bag and head off into the cemetery. After what he'd just been through, he was ready for some Owlboy action.

"Hey, running boy," his mother called.

He was halfway up the back porch steps when he had to stop.

"Give us a hand here with Aunt Tilley's stuff, would you?"

Billy went back down, feeling his sudden burst of energy dwindling.

Dad had opened the trunk to reveal a ton of stuff.

"I thought she was just staying for the weekend, not the next ten years," Billy muttered under his breath as he hauled out one suitcase, then another.

"You boys be careful with those things," Aunt Tilley said as she and his mom strolled arm in arm into the house. "I wouldn't want you to strain your backs."

It took three trips to empty the trunk of Aunt Tilley's weekend necessities, but finally it was over, and Billy was ready to go. Darting into his bedroom and avoiding the obstacle course in it, he grabbed his book bag from the closet and was down the stairs, in the kitchen and almost out the door.

Almost.

"Don't be gone too long," his mother called out. "We're having a special dinner for Aunt Tilley tonight."

He agreed not to be late and was finally able to escape. Over the wall and in the cemetery, he ran toward the Sprylock family mausoleum, content that in a matter of minutes, he would be away from his house and in Monstros City.

Where he wouldn't have to hear about, think about or see *any* old people.

CHAPTER FOUR

"**W**hat do you mean we're going to the old goblins' home?"

Billy had barely had a chance to ask what was going on in Monstros before Archebold had rushed him into the passenger seat of the Owlmobile.

They were already on the move, a snickering Halifax waving to them from the safety of the garage as they departed with a roar of the engine and a screech of tires.

"When you were talking about your great-aunt and stuff, it made me feel kind of guilty about not visiting my grandpa," Archebold said, pudgy hands clasped on the Owlmobile's steering wheel. "And seeing how things are quiet . . . *voilà!*"

Billy leaned his head back against the headrest.

"Why do I have to go?" he whined.

"Because he wanted to meet you," the goblin explained. "All his goblin pals at Groaning Acres—"

"Groaning Acres?" Billy asked.

"Yeah, what's wrong with Groaning Acres?"

"Nothing, go on," Billy told him. "So, he wanted to meet me?"

"Yeah," Archebold went on. "He was one of the reasons I came up to the human world to look for a new Owlboy in the first place."

"Great," Billy muttered. "More old people."

"Goblins," Archebold said, correcting him.

"Yeah, right. But they're still old."

"Got me there," Archebold said.

Large and menacing, Groaning Acres squatted like a prehistoric horned toad on the top of a hill overlooking a portion of the sprawling city. It was covered with windows and steeples and had a huge porch that encircled the front. To Billy it looked almost alive, glaring at him with its many eyelike windows as the Owlmobile drove up the snaking road, through the gate, to park at the front of the establishment.

There were old goblins everywhere. Some were wandering around the building, while many sat in rocking chairs all along the long front porch.

"Hey, Gramps!" Archebold called up to the porch as he climbed from the Owlmobile.

Billy stood beside the passenger door, watching as a goblin wearing a brightly colored Hawaiian shirt, Bermuda shorts, black socks and sandals got up from his rocking chair and began to wave.

"That's him?" Billy asked, joining his friend as they climbed the stairs up to the porch.

"That's him," Archebold said. "That's Grandpa Artemus, the last person to see the previous Owlboy before he disappeared, and one snappy dresser."

Billy couldn't agree more. He practically needed sunglasses to look head-on at the old goblin's Hawaiian shirt.

"Who are the other three?" Billy asked as he stared at three other old goblins, who were seated where Archebold's grandfather had been.

"Those are his buddies," Archebold explained. "The sidekick's sidekicks. Their names are Saul, Percy and Morty."

"There's my Archie!" Grandpa Artemus called out, wrapping his arms around the younger goblin in a powerful hug, then kissing the top of his lumpy head. "Why has it been so long since you've come for a visit?" The old goblin then hit his grandson's head with a loud smack.

"Ow!" Archebold cried. "I've been really busy, Gramps," he explained, rubbing the area where he'd been hit. "Or haven't you noticed who I brought with me?"

The old goblin squinted at Billy, then reached into the front pocket of his shirt and removed a pair of black-framed glasses. He slipped them onto his wide face, his eyes magnified to twice their normal size.

"Well, well, well," Grandpa Artemus said. "It's been a long time since I've seen that costume." He turned to the three goblins sitting in their rocking chairs behind him.

"Hey, fellas, get a load of this." He directed a short, fat finger toward Billy.

Two of the goblins leaned forward in their chairs while the other didn't do much of anything. He was just cobweb-covered goblin bones propped up in the chair.

"Been a long time," said one of Artemus's friends.

"Real long," said the other.

The goblin skeleton suddenly coughed, a blast of dust exploding from his mouth.

Billy jumped, startled by the sight.

"That's Morty," Archebold whispered in Billy's ear. "He's the oldest goblin here, and was assistant to the very first Owlboy."

"Wow," Billy said as Grandpa Artemus and his friends continued to stare at him.

"So you guys knew the other Owlboys," Billy said with awe. "The ones before me?"

All the goblins nodded—except for Morty. He just coughed again, filling the air with a dusty cloud.

"It was the saddest thing when my Owlboy went missing," Grandpa Artemus recalled. The old goblin's eyes filled with tears behind his glasses. "Still chokes me up today."

Saul and Percy got out of their chairs and came to stand behind their friend, comforting him with pats on the back.

"But there's no need to cry anymore, no sir," Grandpa Artemus said, pulling a flowered handkerchief from the back pocket of his Bermuda shorts and wiping the tears beneath his glasses. "No sir, 'cause we've got a new Owlboy now."

Archebold threw his arm around Billy. "Yep, and I found him."

Grandpa Artemus smiled and slowly nodded. "A little small," he said. "But I've been hearing good things."

The other goblins nodded also.

"Good things that would make all the other Owlboys before you proud."

Billy smiled. "Thanks. That means a lot coming from you."

Grandpa Artemus continued to stare at him, rubbing his short, fat fingers along his wrinkled chin.

"What's wrong, Gramps?" Archebold asked. "Is his helmet on crooked or something?" He grabbed Billy by the arms and spun him around for a look. "He seems all right to me."

"He looks fine, Archie," Artemus agreed. "Better than fine, really, which has got me thinking."

"About what?" Billy asked.

"I'm thinking you might be the one," the old goblin said.

His goblin pals started to nod again, as though they understood exactly what he was talking about.

But Billy was still in the dark.

"The one for what?"

Grandpa Artemus squinted behind the thick lenses of his glasses. "The one to find out what happened to him," the old-timer said, his voice a dry whisper. "To solve the mystery of the last Owlboy's disappearance."

Klot stretched his long, spindly arm around the side of the porch, pointing a large plastic ear toward the old goblins' conversation with Owlboy and his sidekick.

"Are you hearing this?" Klot asked excitedly, stretching to be sure that the giant ear would catch it all. He fiddled with the controls on a battery pack attached to his waist.

Klot was wearing headphones, as was Mukus.

"All I'm hearing is the ball game," Mukus said with a smile. "The Monstros City Mutants versus the Monstros City Massacres. The Mutants are kicking their butts!"

Klot tore the headphones from his partner's bulbous head. "They're not the only ones who are going to get their butts kicked once the Monarch hears what I just heard."

The two started to skulk away from Groaning Acres, not wanting to risk being discovered.

"What did you hear?" Mukus asked.

Klot shared his information, and the two of them returned to their master with fear growing in their hearts.

Again they had bad news, and again they feared for their safety.

It called for quick thinking—something to defuse the explosive situation—and Klot thought of just the thing.

"Flowers?" Mukus asked as they walked through the darkness of the tunnel toward the Monarch's secret lair. "You think flowers are going to keep him from being furious?"

Klot nodded, sniffing the black roses with his pointed red nose. "I think they'll do just that," he said. "How can you get mad at somebody who's brought you beautiful flowers? Personally, I think I'm a genius."

"Oh yeah, you're a genius, all right," Mukus scoffed. The rotund, dripping monster shook his head, ooze falling from him like thick drops of smelly rain. "The master criminal of Monstros City is just going to melt over the fact that you brought him flowers."

Klot snarled, looking at his partner. "Well, what would you suggest?"

Mukus pulled a pretty, heart-shaped box from behind his back. "Chocolates, you moron," he said, shaking the red foil box. "Everybody knows that you can't stay mad at somebody who gives you delicious chocolates."

The giant mechanical rat was waiting to escort them to the Monarch's lair. Both of them were eager to award their gifts to their soon-to-be-angry master.

"What is that you're holding?" the Monarch asked from his throne. He pointed to Klot.

"Oh, they're flowers, master," Klot said with an embarrassed smile. "When I saw them, I thought of you."

The red-skinned monster walked quickly over to the hooded figure and laid the bouquet in his lap.

"They're . . . they're lovely," the Monarch said, bringing the flowers up to his hood to sniff. "And they smell wonderful. Thank you, Klot. That was very considerate."

Mukus couldn't stand to see his friend getting all the attention.

"And I thought of you when I saw these," the slimy-skinned creature said, holding up the red heart-shaped box. "Because you're all heart."

The Monarch laughed.

"For me as well?" he asked with disbelief as he took the chocolates from his other lackey. "What did I do to deserve such attention?" he asked.

"We thought you should probably get something to make you happy, since we've got such bad news to tell you," Klot answered without thinking. "Whoops, that just came out."

"Nice," Mukus said.

"Bad news?" the Monarch asked, menace growing in his low, reverberating voice. "What sort of bad news?"

"Well," Klot began, choosing his words carefully, "remember how you told us to follow Owlboy, and to keep you up to date on what he's doing?"

"Yes," the Monarch answered.

"We did just as you asked," Mukus chimed in. "And, well, we found out something that we don't think you're going to like."

The Monarch stood, box of chocolates hanging from one hand, bouquet of flowers from the other.

"Tell me," he demanded.

"We think he's going to start to investigate the mysterious disappearance of the last Owlboy."

The two immediately closed their eyes, both expecting to be pummeled by the fury of their master's rage.

Instead, the Monarch tossed the chocolates and the flowers to the floor, then turned away and stomped off toward a hidden passage that had opened in the wall.

The secret door slid silently shut behind the criminal mastermind.

Klot slowly opened one bloodshot eye and then the other. "Hey; he's gone," the red-skinned monster said, slapping his chubby friend's arm.

Mukus opened his eyes. "Can you believe it? We're not dead," he observed happily.

Klot grinned, ecstatic that they hadn't been destroyed by their master's anger.

Suddenly the secret door slid open, and the Monarch emerged.

"YEEEEEEEEEEEEEEEEK!" the lackeys screamed, Mukus leaping up into Klot's arms.

The crime boss walked around his throne and toward them. Then he stopped, bending down to retrieve the box of chocolates and the flowers.

"Forgot these," he said softly before turning to go back.

The door to his secret room closed behind him with a snakelike hiss.

"You can put me down now," Mukus said.

*   *   *

"What are they doing again?" Billy asked Archebold.

When Billy had agreed with Grandpa Artemus that it would be a great idea to investigate the previous Owl-boy's disappearance, the old goblin and his buddies had suddenly gone into action, getting all excited about showing him their *stuff*.

Whatever the heck that meant.

"You heard him," Archebold said, sounding almost bored. "They're showing you their stuff."

"I don't understand what that . . ."

"They want to show you that they've still got it," Archebold explained. "That they have what it takes to be a superhero's sidekick."

All Billy could do was stare.

They had followed the old goblins out to the back of Groaning Acres, to what looked like an obstacle course of some kind. Before Billy could even ask, the old gob-lins were running the course.

"Maybe they should stop," Billy suggested, watching as one of Artemus's friends—Billy thought that his name was Saul—fell over the side of a climbing wall and landed in a groaning heap on the ground. "I don't want them to hurt themselves."

Archebold waved the thought away. "It'd be like talking to a rock," he said. "They do this every time I come to visit. Now with you here, they're showing off big-time."

Grandpa Artemus helped Saul get to his feet, brushing off the front of the old goblin's baggy pants.

Percy wheeled the bony Morty over to them in his wheelchair.

"Goblin pyramid!" Grandpa Artemus screamed as the goblins all shuffled into action.

Percy climbed onto Morty's chair and held out his hand for Saul to use to climb up onto his shoulders.

Billy winced, but the old goblin managed to make it onto his friend's shoulders.

Then it was Grandpa Artemus's turn. The old goblin dragged a springboard over and positioned it in front of his friends.

"I used to be able to do this without the springboard," he called over his shoulder, getting ready to jump.

"This isn't going to be pretty," Archebold said, putting his hand over his eyes.

Grandpa Artemus ran up, jumped and landed on the springboard, temporarily weighing it down before it sprang back, sending the old goblin flying through the air at his friends.

Billy almost believed that the old-timer was going to make it, but he came down a little low, hitting Saul squarely in the chest and knocking him backward.

So much for a goblin pyramid, Billy thought, watching

as the old goblins wound up in a moaning pile on the ground.

"Is it over yet?" Archebold asked, peeking out through splayed fingers.

"Oh yeah, it's over," Billy said. "Do you think we should help them?"

"Naw," his goblin friend replied. "Like I said, they do this stuff all the time."

Grandpa Artemus, Saul and Percy stiffly climbed to their feet, each of them clutching a piece of Morty's skeleton. The cobweb-covered goblin's chair had flipped over as well, scattering his bones.

The old goblins immediately started putting their buddy back together. They righted Morty's chair and lovingly placed their skeletal pal back into his seat.

Morty coughed loudly, his jaw falling away from his skull. Saul carefully reattached it, patting the ancient goblin on the top of his head.

"So, what do you think, Billy?" Grandpa Artemus asked, walking over to him. "Do we still got it or what?"

"You got it, all right," Billy answered with a polite smile.

"Maybe one of these days, if you find yourself in a fix, you'll give us a call and we can lend a hand. What do ya think?"

"Sure," Billy answered. "Goblins of your talents

would be really useful, I bet." He looked at Archebold. "Don't you think?"

"I'm going to the car," the goblin said with a shake of his head. He turned and walked from the yard.

"I guess he agrees," Billy said with a shrug.

The old goblins started to cheer and gave each other high fives.

They were so caught up in their excitement that they didn't even notice Billy leaving.

CHAPTER FIVE

Billy slowly raised the forkful of his mother's special lasagna to his mouth as Aunt Tilley continued talking.

"And Gertrude said that she'd never seen a bunion quite so big and had to make an appointment with the podiatrist the very next morning."

She had been going on like this for hours now. Billy felt as though his brain had been injected with a big needle of novocaine.

"Podiatrist?" he asked.

"The foot doctor," his mother said with a polite smile as she wiped her mouth with her napkin.

"That's right," Aunt Tilley said with a huge smile. "The finest foot doctor in all of Massachusetts. He helped me with the corns I had back in '87."

She paused briefly, thinking about her corns, Billy imagined. Foolishly, he thought they might be in for a reprieve.

So far, Aunt Tilley had talked about everything from the high prices of coffee and toilet tissue to her best friend, Edna, whose daughter married a man who had invented an edible dental floss and who was supposed to be on Oprah but got sick with a flu that made all his hair fall out.

There was more—much more—but he couldn't bring himself to remember.

Billy chewed his food, enjoying the sudden silence. By the looks of relief on his parents' faces, he could tell they were enjoying it as well.

Suddenly Aunt Tilley made a bizarre sound—a weird clicking noise.

He was about to ask her if she was all right when she reached up and plucked her false teeth from her mouth.

"Excuse me," she said, grabbing her napkin and rubbing her choppers.

Whatever the problem was, it was fixed, and she slid the dentures back in, then moved her mouth around until they popped into place.

"There," she said, a huge smile spreading across her old face, showing off the artificial teeth. "Much better. Now, where was I?"

Billy almost screamed.

"That's right," Aunt Tilley said, remembering. "My corns."

Mom and Dad immediately got to their feet, plates in hand. It was as if some sort of code word that Billy wasn't privy to had been spoken. They went to the sink and busied themselves with cleaning their plates.

But Aunt Tilley didn't miss a beat, looking right at Billy, her eyes rendering him motionless. He wanted to get up as well—to run screaming from the kitchen— but he couldn't. The story of how bad the corns on her feet had been seemed to act like another dose of the numbing medicine to his already unfeeling brain.

"More novocaine, Mr. Hooten?"

"Why, of course!"

"Would you like another cup of tea, Aunt Tilley?" Mom asked as she placed her plate into the dish strainer.

"Oh yes, dear," Aunt Tilley answered. "That would be lovely."

Billy saw this as his opportunity. Shaking off the effects of brain death, he picked up his plate and started to stand.

He almost made it.

"So, how's school, Billy?" Aunt Tilley asked as she took the cup and saucer from his mother.

Billy was frozen by his great-aunt's words. He looked

to his mother for help, but she just smiled, taking his dirty plate.

Better you than me, her eyes said.

"I can remember when you were born. You were only a little thing, but you had the most enormous head."

It's like being in the presence of a new supervillain, Billy thought as she continued to drone on, pausing only momentarily—not long enough for him to escape—to take a little sip of her tea. *The Talker.*

Aunt Tilley was on her third cup of tea and taking a rest in the midst of her latest discussion, the topic of which was figuring out the puzzling reason Billy didn't have a girlfriend, when he saw his opportunity.

"Hey, why don't we go see what's on TV?"

His parents had already beat feet into the living room as soon as they'd finished with the dishes, leaving him there alone with the chattering Aunt Tilley . . . *the Talker.*

"Oh, that might be nice," she said with a pleasant smile that showed no sign of the true villainy hidden behind her flapping gums. "What night is this again?"

"It's Saturday," Billy said, quickly getting up from his chair and avoiding eye contact just in case she came up with something new to go on and on about.

Billy entered the living room ahead of his aunt. They had brought down a rocking chair from upstairs for her; it was one of the few items that didn't get stuck in his room.

His parents were in their usual places: Mom on the couch, Dad in his recliner.

"There's your seat over there, Auntie," Billy said, pointing to the rocker.

"How nice," she said, making her way toward the rocking chair.

He'd wanted to get out that night for some Owlboy action, and normally would have just waited until both parents were asleep, but with Aunt Tilley there, there was a wrinkle in the way he would normally do things. He had no idea if his aunt was affected by television— or the Sleep Machine, as he liked to call it—the way his folks were.

He might need to wait a bit and observe before he planned his evening routine.

As Aunt Tilley slowly lowered herself into her seat, Billy turned to see what his parents were watching. If he was going to have to wait awhile before going out, he hoped it was something good.

Somebody wearing rubber gloves was pulling a grasshopper from somebody else's nostril.

"Awesome!" Billy said, plopping his butt down on the floor. "I love this show."

"What is this?" Aunt Tilley asked.

Billy turned around and saw that his aunt was wearing a look of absolute disgust.

"It's CSC," Billy answered, but he could see that she still didn't get it. *Crime Scene Cleanup,*" he explained further. "This show is awesome."

The grasshopper removed from the dead guy's nose was now being examined by the crack team of crime scene cleaner-uppers; Billy couldn't wait to find out why and how the bug had got up there.

"Is there something you'd like to watch, Aunt Tilley?" Billy's dad suddenly asked.

Shocked, Billy turned to his father. "But, Dad . . . the grasshopper in the nose!"

"Aunt Tilley's company, Billy," Dad explained. "And we should be doing everything possible to make her feel at home."

"You can see a grasshopper stuck up somebody's nose any old time," Mom said from the couch. She wasn't even watching; she was doing one of her Sudoku puzzles.

"Oh, I'd hate to turn the channel if Billy's watching this," Aunt Tilley said, looking right at him.

He knew that CSC wasn't for everybody, and besides, if what she wanted to watch was boring enough, maybe they would all fall asleep and he would be able to sneak out of the house that much more quickly.

"That's all right, Auntie. I've already seen this one anyway," he lied. "You can watch whatever you want."

Billy grabbed the remote. "What channel do you want?"

The old woman smiled, starting to rock happily in her chair. "I really enjoy what's on channel twenty-nine," she said.

"Channel twenty-nine it is," Billy said, pointing the remote at the TV and pushing the buttons.

The channel changed to a guy and a lady dressed in crazy spangly outfits and doing some weird dance as an audience cheered them on.

"Is this what you want?" Billy asked incredulously.

"This is it," Aunt Tilley said with obvious excitement.

"What is it?"

"*Polkaing with the Famous.*" Aunt Tilley clapped her hands to the music. "It wouldn't be Saturday night at Shady Acres without it."

"What . . . what are they doing?" Billy asked, unable to take his eyes off the screen.

"That's the polka," Aunt Tilley answered. "Uncle Freddy and I used to love to dance the polka."

"So is this some sort of contest?"

"Oh yes, celebrities compete for the title of Polka Master and for valuable prizes. It's very exciting," Aunt Tilley explained.

Billy continued to watch, looking for celebrities, but he didn't see any. There was a guy he vaguely remembered from a show about a truck driver with a pet orangutan, but that was the closest to a celebrity that he saw.

He wished that the orangutan were on the show instead; Billy would have paid good money to see him dance the polka.

Billy looked at his parents. Dad was fast asleep, and so was Mom. It was just Billy and Aunt Tilley and *Polkaing with the Famous*.

Billy wondered if it was possible for a television program to melt somebody's brain.

He wasn't sure how long he had sat, paralyzed in front of the television as one after another of Aunt Tilley's favorite shows dragged by.

He was about to start watching one about an old lady and her pet pig who solved mysteries in a small farming community in Kansas when he mustered the strength to turn his head away from the screen.

"I think I'm going to bed," Billy said, his voice lacking all hints of energy.

"But don't you want to see who poisoned Farmer Flaherty's chickens?" Aunt Tilley asked with wonder.

"No . . . not really," he said, struggling to stand after

what seemed like fourteen days. In fact it had been only an hour and a half.

Mom and Dad were snoring away, oblivious to what he had just endured.

Billy approached his aunt and gave her a quick kiss on the cheek. "Good night," he said.

"Good night, Billy." She gave him a kiss even though her eyes were glued to the television set. It appeared that the pig was about to uncover a very important clue in the chicken-poisoning investigation.

"I'm not planning on being up that much longer. As soon as this is over, I'm off to bed," Aunt Tilley said.

Good, Billy thought as he headed for the stairs. With Aunt Tilley in her room, and Mom and Dad asleep in the living room, he would have the perfect opportunity to sneak out to Monstros.

Halfway up the stairs he realized how tired he was. His legs felt as though somebody had filled his bones with lead. It had been a very long time since he'd gotten up bright and early that morning.

Maybe I'll take a little nap before I head out, he thought. Just enough rest to give him his second wind. That would do the trick.

He stood in the doorway to his room, looking over the mounds, stacks and piles of stuff from the junk room, and wondered if he had the strength to make it to his bed. He did, and he kicked off his sneakers, sitting on the edge of the mattress. He would lie down for a few minutes, just until Aunt Tilley went to bed. And then, when the coast was finally clear, it would be time for superhero action.

At least, that was what he told himself as he lay back on the bed, falling fast asleep before his head even hit the pillow.

CHAPTER SIX

The screeching winds blowing off Mount Terror—in the Abomination Mountain Range—nearly knocked Klot and Mukus from their precarious perch on an icy ledge.

"It's fr-fr-freezing up here," Mukus complained, pulling the hood of his heavy jacket more tightly around his round face. "It's ma-ma-making my slime freeze."

Klot braced himself against the side of the cliff as he pulled a map from inside his coat pocket.

"It shouldn't be too far," he said, studying the detailed directions the Monarch had given him. He glanced up from their perch, trying to find some landmarks, but the distance was lost in the swirling wind and snow.

"I don't care how far it is," Mukus argued, setting down the heavy pack that he had worn on his back all the way up the mountain face. "I'm freezing and I need a hat. . . . This hood isn't . . ."

The chubby monster unzipped the pack in search of something warmer for his head.

"YEEEK!" Mukus squealed as a peeper-fruit-sized mechanical eye floated up from inside the pack.

"Have you reached your designated destination?" the Monarch's voice asked from a tiny speaker located in the body of the mechanized orb.

"Not quite yet, master," Klot stated, shoving the directions back into his pocket.

"Why not?" the Monarch asked. "Don't you realize how important this is for our plans to destroy the hated do-gooder Owlboy once and for all?"

"We do, honestly, sir, but we still have a bit of a climb ahead of us before we can—"

"Useless," the Monarch growled, the machine tilting itself upward to see what remained of their trek. "If I had better lackeys, my master plan would have been in full swing already."

Klot glanced at Mukus, and they both hung their heads, ashamed that they weren't the villains they should be.

"It looks like I'm going to have to help you if I want my plans to ever be carried out," the Monarch sighed from the floating eye.

A tiny hatch on the side of the orb slid open with a

hum, and a spindly mechanical arm with a nozzle at its end unfolded from inside.

"Stay still," the Monarch commanded. "I only have the battery power to do this once."

The pair looked at each other again and were about to ask the question *Do what once?* when twin rays of scarlet energy shot from the end of the nozzle with a high-pitched buzzing.

The two monsters gasped as they were each struck by the beams of crimson energy and slowly lifted from the ground.

"I don't like this!" Mukus squealed, his squat legs kicking as he floated upward.

"Stop that squirming at once!" the Monarch commanded.

Klot reached out and grabbed his partner's shoulder and the two continued their ascent through the whipping snow.

"Don't look down," Klot told his friend after experiencing a brief glimpse of how far he would fall if his master's levitation beam were suddenly to fail. "You really don't want to look down."

"I'm not looking down," Mukus said, squeezing his eyes tightly closed.

The Monarch's mechanical eye followed the pair upward and set them down on an ice-encrusted ledge before the mouth of a cave.

"Is it safe?" Mukus asked, refusing to open his eyes until he was certain.

Klot steeled himself, then opened his red-rimmed eyes.

"It's safe," he said, nudging his pal.

The spindly arm disappeared back inside the body of the eye. "Now, go inside," the orb ordered. "There is much to do before the wheels of chaos are set in motion."

The two entered the darkness of the cave with the mechanical eye floating behind them.

"I can't see a thing," Klot said, Mukus crashing into his back as Klot stopped short.

There was another whirring sound from the body of the orb, and a beam of light illuminated the icy chamber.

"Much better," Klot said as he looked around.

"This way," the eye ordered, floating into a snaking passage that had more twists and turns than the large intestine of a Mega-gigantisaur.

The winding corridor came to an end at a short ledge just before a sudden drop into a vast cavern so deep that the nether regions were lost in total darkness.

"This is it," the Monarch said, the eye hovering over the chasm and making an attempt to peer down, down, down into the darkness below.

A strange rumbling bubbled up from somewhere at the cavern's bottom.

"What's that?" Mukus asked, holding on to Klot as he peered over the edge.

"I don't have a clue," Klot answered, firmly planting his feet to avoid being pulled over the ledge by his curious friend.

"It is the sound that signals the beginning of the end for our most hated enemy," the Monarch growled. "Prepare the awakenator."

Mukus and Klot stared at one another before looking back at the eye.

"The awakenator! The awakenator!" the Monarch screamed. "Inside your bags . . . the instruments that you lugged for most of your journey up Mount Terror!"

"Oh, this junk?" Mukus said, taking off his backpack and dumping the machine parts onto the ground.

Klot did the same, adding the contents of his pack to Mukus' pile.

The two then knelt down in front of the parts and began the slow process of assembling the awakenator.

With the floating orb's assistance—two tiny metal arms that ended in tiny metal fingers had emerged from inside the mechanical eye's housing—the strange device was completed.

Mukus and Klot stood staring at the machine, their hands on their hips.

"So, that's the awakenator, huh?" Klot said.

"Looks like an alarm clock," Mukus added, pointing to the circular face of the device with the large bell-like mechanisms that protruded from each side.

The Monarch's eye floated down to the front of the awakenator, more spindly arms emerging from inside the orb, pushing buttons and flipping switches on the clocklike device.

"How perceptive you've become, Mukus," the Monarch whispered, busily adjusting some knobs. "You've managed to evolve from idiot to moron in a matter of seconds. Good show. The less said about Klot, the better."

Mukus smacked his buddy's shoulder proudly. "Did you hear that? I'm a moron now. Put that in your pipe and smoke it."

Klot looked sad, his shoulders drooping.

"That's not fair. I want to be a moron too."

The Monarch's voice chuckled over the speaker of the mechanized eye. "And I'm sure you'll achieve that lofty goal eventually," he said. "But now is not the time. We must focus all our attention on achieving our goal of destroying he who wishes to take away all that I have worked so hard to acquire."

"That's Owlboy . . . right?" Klot asked nervously.

"Congratulations, Klot. You are finally what you aspired to be," the Monarch said dryly. "You are a moron."

Klot shot his long arms up into the air. "Yes!"

"I was a moron first," Mukus grumbled, crossing his arms over his chubby chest. "You just remember that."

"Enough!" the Monarch scolded. "Prepare to activate the awakenator!"

The monsters stood tensed, not knowing what they should be doing.

One of the orb's mechanical limbs extended down from the body of the eye to point out a button that was flashing red.

"Activate the awakenator," the Monarch said again.

Both Klot and Mukus lunged for the button.

The chamber was suddenly filled with a horrible ringing. Mukus's and Klot's hands immediately went to their ears, but it did little to protect them from the deafening racket.

The eye drifted closer to them. "Earplugs," the Monarch said.

"What?" Klot screamed. "I can't hear you."

Mukus nudged his buddy. "Maybe we should use these earplugs," he screamed, pulling the bright orange ear stoppers from his pocket and waving them in front of his friend's face.

Klot gave Mukus the thumbs-up, fishing his own earplugs from his pocket, and the two stuck them into their ears.

"Much better," Klot said, turning his attention back to the Monarch's eye. "Now, what did you say, boss?"

"Never mind," the eye said, floating out over the chasm.

Suddenly the cave chamber was filled with an even louder sound, followed by a tremendous shock wave that sent powerful vibrations through the ledge.

"Wha-wha-what was that?" Mukus asked, clutching at his buddy's arm.

"I don't know," Klot said. He looked to the eye for some answers.

Something deep below, in the darkness of the cavern, roared even more loudly than before, the vibrations causing icy chunks of the cave ceiling to rain down on them.

"The awakenator has done its job," the Monarch's eye proclaimed. "*He* has been awakened."

Klot and Mukus, holding each other in fear, peered over the ledge at the darkness. Something was moving.

Something big.

"Who—who has been awakened?" Mukus asked.

The roar came again, and they watched in horror as a gigantic hand reached out from the ocean of darkness below.

"YAAARRRRRRRRRGH!" Mukus and Klot screamed in unison.

"The great terror has awakened," the Monarch proclaimed proudly. "The terror that is Zis-Boom-Bah!"

The country-fried bat wings are especially tasty today, Archebold thought as he leaned back in his recliner in front of the multiple television screens in the monitoring room inside the Roost.

He was reading the latest issue of the *Monstros Inquisitor*—catching up on all the gossip in the burg of beasts—when the warning alarms started to clang noisily.

"What's that all about?" he asked, pushing a particularly large bat wing into his open mouth, his eyes never leaving the story he was reading in the magazine.

Halifax was sitting on his portable folding chair on the other side of the room, magazine in his lap, enjoying some chocolate-covered leeches with a cold bottle of Bloodweiser Beetle Brew Beer.

"I don't know," he said without looking up. "Sounds like an alarm." He licked a fat, stubby troll finger before turning the page.

Exasperated, Archebold looked at the maintenance troll. "You're gonna make me get up, aren't you?"

"I didn't say you had to get up," the troll answered, holding the magazine up to his face for a closer look.

Archebold tossed his magazine onto the table beside him and got down from his chair, grumbling under his breath. The alarm was still ringing loudly, and the goblin wasn't sure if he'd ever heard this particular alarm before.

"That's a different sound, don't you think?" he asked, moving closer to the monitors, searching for a sign of trouble.

"Sounds old," Halifax said, his shaggy face still buried in his magazine. "Maybe one of the earliest alarms installed."

Archebold moved even closer to the multiple screens, looking for the source of the incessant pealing. "I just can't see where the problem is," the goblin said.

Halifax looked up with a sigh. "I knew I was gonna have to get up," he said. The troll stood, throwing his magazine down on the seat.

"I can't find it," Archebold said. "From what I can see, everything looks copasetic."

Halifax sidled up next to him. "Let me see," he said. He took a pair of filthy glasses from inside the front pocket of his overalls and stuck them on his hairy face.

"Suit yourself," Archebold said, crossing his arms over his chest. "I've looked at every screen and I can't find the bother."

The alarm continued to toll, and Archebold knew

that if they didn't stop it soon, he was going to have one mother of a headache.

The troll stepped back from the screens. He removed his glasses and slipped them back into his pocket.

"See? I told you," Archebold chided, certain that Halifax hadn't found the source of the alarm either.

"I was right about the alarm," the troll said, walking past him toward a control panel in the wall. "It is an old one . . . and it's connected to an old screen."

"Which one?" Archebold asked, his eyes again scanning the monitors.

"An old one," Halifax said. He unsnapped a latch and pulled open the control panel. Beside the switches that ran power to the various pieces of machinery in the monitor room, there was a flashing green light and a switch beneath it.

The troll flicked the switch. There was a grinding sound, followed by a soft vibration.

Archebold watched as the center television monitors started to move to either side, revealing another, larger screen beneath.

"Would you look at that?" the goblin said. "Why is that one under there?"

"It used to be important a long, long time ago. It required constant monitoring. I guess when it didn't need to be watched as much, it just got covered up."

The screen was layered with dust, but Archebold could still see the peaks of Mount Terror in the Abomination Mountain Range.

"Hey, wait a sec. I know that place," he said.

"Yep, we all do . . . and if you don't, you should," the troll said. "That was where one of the very first Owlboys defeated one of the greatest threats ever in the history of Monstros City."

Archebold slowly nodded in agreement. "They kept a camera on it just to make sure that the threat never came back."

They stood in silence, staring at the cold- and foreboding-looking mountain range.

"Wonder why the alarm . . . ," Archebold began, but never finished.

A section of Mount Terror's front suddenly started to crumble, breaking away.

Archebold and Halifax both gasped as they watched something huge emerge from within the hollowed-out section of Mount Terror, roaring to the heavens as it pushed rock, dirt, snow and ice aside so that it could be free.

"It's Zis-Boom-Bah," Archebold said, barely able to breathe.

"I know it's Zis-Boom-Bah," Halifax answered in a high-pitched voice that dripped with terror.

"We need Billy," Archebold said, his eyes fixed on the horror unfolding before him. "We need Owlboy."

"And we need him right away."

Billy couldn't believe that he'd fallen asleep with his clothes on.

Aunt Tilley's shows must've done more damage than he'd originally thought.

He grabbed his book bag with his Owlboy costume inside and headed for the door. It was still early enough that no one would be up, which was perfect for a little Owlboy action before breakfast.

Carefully, he opened his door and tiptoed out into the hall. He was just about to go down the stairs when he heard the upstairs toilet flush and the bathroom door open.

Nabbed.

Aunt Tilley smiled when she saw him, and his plans to get out to Monstros early shattered like glass.

"I thought I was the only one awake," she whispered, pulling her bathrobe belt more tightly around her slight frame. Aunt Tilley shuffled toward him. "Let's go downstairs so we don't wake up your mom and dad."

She put an arm around Billy's shoulders as the two of

them descended the stairs and headed for the kitchen. Aunt Tilley went right to the table and sat down.

Billy simply stood in the middle of the room, book bag in hand. He didn't know what to do. No way did he want a repeat of the night before. He wasn't sure his brain could take it.

"It seems like a lovely morning," the old woman said finally, craning her neck to see out the window over the kitchen sink.

"Yeah, I guess," Billy said, looking outside for the first time that morning. For all he'd known, it could've been raining.

He didn't want to just leave her sitting there all alone. It would make him feel guilty.

"Would you like something?" he asked, not knowing what else to say. "I could make you some cereal or something."

"I would love a cup of tea if it's not a bother," she said.

Billy grabbed the teakettle off the stove and began to fill it at the sink.

"My mother always said that a nice cup of tea is the perfect way to start the day," Aunt Tilley began.

Billy felt his strength begin to waver as she started to talk. He knew that this story would flow into another, followed by another, and another one after that.

Trapped again.

His aunt was in the middle of a story—about how many cups of tea her mother used to have in a day, and how she lived to be ninety-nine years old—when she suddenly stopped talking.

The silence was almost deafening. Billy turned the water off and turned toward his aunt, kettle still in hand, worried that maybe she'd had a coronary. His parents always talked about old people having coronaries, whatever that meant.

He was relieved to see that she was just sitting, although it made him a little nervous, because she seemed to be staring right through him.

"I do go on sometimes, don't I?" she said with a nervous laugh.

Yes, yes, you do. You go on and on and on and on and on into infinity, Billy wanted to say, but he knew that that would be mean.

"Oh, I don't know," he said, taking the teakettle to the stove and placing it on the burner. "I really didn't notice."

He didn't know what had made her say that. He hoped that he hadn't made an evil face or something when she'd started talking. That would have been mean too.

"That should only take a couple of minutes," he said, turning from the stove to face Aunt Tilley again.

She looked a little sad.

"What's wrong, Auntie?" he asked, suddenly feeling guilty. "Did I do something to hurt your feelings?"

Aunt Tilley smiled. "Not at all, Billy," she said, pulling out the chair beside her and patting it for him to sit down.

He did, trying not to sigh as he sat.

"I just want you to know that I'm sorry if I talk too much," she said as she placed her warm, dry hand over his. "When you get to be my age, you lose an awful lot."

"Like Uncle Fred?" Billy asked, wanting to be sure that he understood where she was coming from.

"Like Uncle Fred," Aunt Tilley repeated with a nod. "It's very hard to be alone, Billy," she continued. "You save up all the conversations that you would've had, and when you have a chance to spend some time with people that you love, it just all comes bubbling out."

The water in the kettle eventually started to boil and Billy got up to make the tea. He brought a steaming mug to the table, suddenly not in such a hurry to run off to Monstros City. There would be plenty of time for that later; after all, it was a long weekend.

He set the cup in front of Aunt Tilley, along with the sugar bowl and a carton of milk. "There ya go," he said, again taking a seat.

"Thank you, Billy," she said as she repeatedly dunked the tea bag in the hot water.

Billy smiled. "So, your mom drank a lot of tea?" he asked with real curiosity. "How much was a lot?"

And Aunt Tilley launched into the story about her mother's tea-drinking habits, and how her father used to scold her mother, saying that there wouldn't be any tea left in the world if she kept on drinking it the way she did.

After a few more stories, Billy made his aunt some toast, and he was having a glass of juice himself when there was a knock at the door.

"Company so early?" Aunt Tilley asked, turning in her seat toward the sound.

Billy walked to the door and looked through the curtain, spying a tiny figure with pigtails standing on the stoop.

Victoria. Who else could it be at this hour? he thought as he pulled open the door.

"Good morning, Vic—" he said, but the rest got stuck in his throat like dry shredded wheat.

He was staring at the ugliest little girl he had ever seen. In fact, she looked like Archebold would if he dressed up like Victoria.

And then it hit him like a ton of bricks: it *was* Archebold dressed up to look like Victoria.

Billy couldn't speak.

"Hi, Billy," Archebold said in a high, girlish voice that was one of the creepiest things Billy had ever had the displeasure of hearing. "Can you come out and play?"

Archebold's goblin eyes were wide as he jerked his head toward the backyard, nearly causing his wig to fly off. He wanted Billy to follow him.

"Who's that, Billy?" Aunt Tilley asked from the kitchen table.

"It's just Victoria," Billy lied. "She lives next door and . . ."

"Invite her in," Aunt Tilley said. "I'd love to meet her. Your mother and father were telling me just the other day how cute she is."

"I don't think that's wise, Auntie," Billy said, trying to dissuade her. "She's really wild and could tear this house apart in seconds and . . ."

Aunt Tilley turned her chair toward the open door.

"Come in here and say hello," she said to the disguised Archebold, motioning for him to come into the house.

Billy let the door open wider to allow Archebold inside.

"Aren't you the cutest little . . . ," Aunt Tilley began, but it seemed she was having a hard time finishing the sentence.

". . . thing," she finally said.

Billy was able to get a good look now at how Archebold was dressed. He had on a shiny silver Barbie jacket with spangles, dark blue dungarees with butterflies on the butt pockets and pink sneakers.

What a sight.

"And how old are you?" Aunt Tilley asked.

"I'll be three hundred and sixteen on the—"

Billy slapped the back of the goblin's head before he could finish.

"Five," Billy said. "She'll be six next December. Right, Victoria?"

Archebold rubbed the back of his head where he'd been smacked, careful not to make his wig crooked.

"Yeah, six. That's right," he agreed.

"Isn't that wonderful." Aunt Tilley said. "And what brings you over here so bright and early this morning?"

She reached out and poked Archebold's belly with her finger.

The goblin did his best little-girl giggle and Billy thought he would lose his mind. It was one of the most disturbing things he'd ever heard.

"I was hoping that Billy would come outside and play with me," Archebold told the old woman.

"Isn't that sweet?" Aunt Tilley said, looking at Billy. She reached out and tickled the goblin. "Then what are you hanging around this kitchen talking with an old fogey like me for when you should be outside playing?" she asked happily.

Archebold giggled some more and Billy felt the hair on the back of his neck stand on end.

He picked up his book bag from where he'd dropped it and pushed the disguised goblin toward the door. "I better take her outside to play before she starts crying or something."

On his way out, Billy kissed Aunt Milley lightly on the cheek. "You're not really alone as long as you have me and my folks," he whispered in her ear before heading out the door—taking the ugliest little girl he'd ever seen with him.

CHAPTER SEVEN

"What is *wrong* with you?" Billy screeched as he and the disguised Archebold headed toward the stone wall that separated his yard from the Pine Hill Cemetery.

"What?" Archebold asked, clearly without a clue.

"How you're dressed," Billy said as he hopped up onto the wall and reached down to give his goblin pal a hand.

"I think I look adorable," Archebold said. "Plus, it was the quickest disguise I could throw together on such short notice. It was either this or a Roman centurion."

They both jumped down into the cemetery and jogged onto the path.

"I guess a Roman centurion would have been even harder to explain to Aunt Tilley," Billy said. "But that

113

doesn't change the fact that you're the ugliest little girl I have ever seen. My aunt's eyeglass prescription must need to be changed or something."

"You're just jealous you don't look as good in a wig," Archebold fired back.

They went inside the Sprylock family mausoleum and Billy started to change.

"So, what's the big deal?" he asked, pulling off his T-shirt and undoing his pants.

Archebold went to the stone coffin and slid the heavy lid over a little more.

"It's bad, Billy," the goblin said. "Really bad."

"All right, what's really bad?" Billy asked, slipping on his Owlboy headpiece and goggles. "Let me in on the secret. If I've got to save the day and everything, what the heck am I going up against?"

They both crawled inside the coffin and began their journey down the stone steps, deep into the darkness.

"Take everything you've already gone up against as Owlboy and multiply it by a gazillion."

"What is it, for Pete's sake!" Billy exclaimed.

Archebold took a really big firefly out of his jacket pocket. Billy could hear the bug snoring loudly as the goblin gave it a good shake.

"Wake up, Walter. I need to see where I'm going," Archebold said.

The bug's butt immediately lit up, shining a helpful glow over the winding stone steps.

"You could have been a little more gentle," Walter complained. "I was asleep."

"Sorry. This is kind of an emergency. I've got to get Billy back right away."

The firefly looked at Billy with large bulbous eyes. "Oh, him," he said with a slight hint of disgust. "What's he gonna do against a threat like that?"

"I wish you'd cut him some slack, Walter," Archebold said. "He's been doing a really good job."

"Yeah, until now," the bug said, jabbing.

Billy came to a sudden stop on the steps.

"All right, that's it," he said, stamping his boot. "Will somebody please explain what I'm about to walk into here? It's the least you could do."

"From the frying pan into the fire," the bug buzzed.

"Quiet, you," Archebold said, giving the large bug another violent shake. "Sorry about that, Billy."

"Please just tell me what's going on. Is Monstros in danger?"

"More so than any other time since you've become Owlboy," the goblin replied.

They started down the steps again, not wanting to waste any time.

"A long time ago, when Monstros was really young,

one of the very first Owlboys saved the city from a gigantic beast called Zis-Boom-Bah."

"You're joking," Billy said. "Zis-Boom-Bah?"

"I wish I were joking," Archebold said. "The monster was huge and hungry, and nearly completely destroyed Monstros in his terrible rampage."

"But Owlboy saved the day, right?" Billy asked. "He always saves the day."

"Yeah, he did, but it was really close," Archebold went on. "If it weren't for some quick thinking, which resulted in Owlboy luring the beast out to the Abomination Mountain Range, and knocking him down into an active volcano, I doubt we'd be standing here today."

They reached the bottom of the steps and, without missing a beat, continued down one of the shadowy paths that would take them to the entrance of the Roost.

"So I'm guessing this Zis-Boom-Bah has found his way out of the volcano."

Archebold looked at him and Billy saw fear in his beady goblin eyes.

"We always suspected that he might, but after so many years we hoped that he wouldn't."

"A lot of good that did," Walter piped up. "Zis-Boom-Bah is back, and the Owlboy who defeated him the first time is long gone."

They reached the door to the Roost, and Archebold turned the knob to let them in.

"But I'm Owlboy now," Billy said with great confidence. "I'm sure I'll think of a way to stop him."

Walter started to laugh. It was a really annoying buzzing sound that came to an abrupt end when Archebold shoved the bug back inside his coat pocket.

"Sorry about that," the goblin said as they entered the Roost.

"That guy really bugs me," Billy grumbled.

"I should probably just buy a flashlight," Archebold observed.

They both walked over to the monitors. Halifax was standing there perfectly still, staring. All the screens were tuned to the Abomination Mountain Range, and Billy got his first good look at the threat he would soon be dealing with.

"There he is," Archebold said, backing up a bit, as if it were dangerous even to get close to the monitors.

Billy stood beside Halifax, also looking at the screens.

"Scared yet?" Halifax suddenly asked.

Billy didn't answer, stunned into silence by what he was looking at.

"Well, if you're not," Halifax went on, "you will be."

Billy had never seen a monster like it.

Zis-Boom-Bah had the furry upper body of some sort

of giant ape, which blended into almost lizardlike skin and legs that could have belonged to a T. rex. He had a tail, too, but it looked like it belonged to some type of fish. And were those bug antennae sticking out of his head?

It was as if somebody had taken a bunch of species, tossed them into a bag and shaken well.

Instant giant monster is served.

The enormous beast was sliding down the face of the mountain, causing a bit of an avalanche as he descended.

"He'll be hitting the Frightening Forest next," Archebold said.

Billy glanced at the goblin and was shocked to see that he'd changed out of his little-girl disguise and into his typical tails.

Both Archebold and Halifax seemed really scared, and Billy wasn't feeling too well at the moment himself, but he was Owlboy now, and he had to do something to make it so that they weren't afraid anymore.

That was what heroes did.

"How's the city dealing with this?" Billy asked.

Halifax took a remote control from a pocket in the front of his dirty overalls and changed the channel on four of the monitors. Monstros City was in a panic; the streets were clogged with abandoned vehicles, and citizens were running around like ants under a magnifying glass.

"That isn't good," Billy said.

"They're scared," Archebold said. "Some of them might even remember the last time."

"I need to talk to them," Billy said. "To let them know that I'm gonna try to stop Zis-Boom-Bah from reaching the city."

Halifax looked away from the television screens for the first time since Billy had got there.

"That would probably go a long way in making them feel better," the troll said. "Especially coming from you."

It was decided. That was what he was going to do.

"I think the Owlcopter would probably be my best bet," Billy said as he left the monitoring station.

Archebold and Halifax followed as he strode with purpose down the corridor toward the elevator. The doors parted and they all clambered inside. Billy jabbed the button that sent the elevator up to the garage.

He was feeling a little bit scared but at the same time excited. This was his first time dealing with a giant monster, and he didn't want to screw things up.

The Owlcopter squatted in the corner, its yellow paint job glowing like a giant canary.

"All right, let's do this," Billy said.

Halifax ran over to a wall panel and opened the

metal door. He immediately began flicking switches, and the front entrance of the Roost's garage began to open.

Archebold climbed into the cockpit with Billy beside him. Halifax crawled in behind the passenger seat and sat down on the floor.

"Here we go," Archebold announced as he hit the ignition switch, and the powerful engine whined to life, the twin rotor blades spinning faster and faster. The bird's head–shaped craft lifted from the garage, flying through the open passage into the night.

Archebold piloted the copter away from the giant tree that was the secret location of the Roost, over the Wailing Wood and toward the city.

"Oh my," Archebold said, looking out his side window at the streets below. They were even more crowded with panicked citizens than before.

Billy reached out to the control panel in front of him and picked up a microphone. "Are we ready?" he asked Halifax.

The troll had opened a small hatch in the belly of the Owlcopter and had lowered a speaker. He gave Billy the thumbs-up as he looked down through the opening at the growing gaggle of monsters in the streets below.

"Citizens of Monstros City," Billy said, his voice booming from the speaker.

Archebold allowed the craft to hover over the crowd.

"This is Owlboy speaking to you from the Owl-copter," Billy said, and suddenly realized that he didn't quite know what to say.

"Ummm . . . how's it going?" he asked.

The crowd reacted with screams, squeals and cries about how scared they were and how Zis-Boom-Bah was coming to destroy them all.

Billy had to do something to put them at ease.

"Don't worry," he said. "Ahhhhh . . . Ummmm . . . I deal with giant monsters all the time. This one shouldn't be any problem . . . I don't think."

"You deal with giant monsters all the time?" Archebold asked, keeping the craft steady over the street. "As if."

"Knock it off. I'm trying to help them relax," Billy said, covering the microphone with his hand.

He continued speaking into the mic.

"So if you want, you can all go home and relax. I'm gonna try to do some stuff and take care of this prob-lem. All right?"

The crowd actually seemed to be calming down a bit.

"Hey, I think it's working," Billy said excitedly.

They all watched from above as the crowds began to disperse, returning to the sidewalks, office buildings and homes. Some returned to their vehicles.

Billy leaned into the back of the copter to give

Halifax a high five. He was feeling pretty good and was glad that he was able to help the situation.

"What's that?" Archebold suddenly asked.

Billy turned around in his seat as Halifax scrambled from the back to peer out the front windshield from between the seats in the cockpit.

"What's what?" Billy asked.

"That brown dot way over there that seems to be getting bigger," the goblin said, tapping on the windshield.

When Billy finally saw what Archebold was trying to point out, it wasn't really a dot anymore; it was bigger and still growing by the second.

Something had been thrown from the vicinity of the Frightening Forest and it was about to have a direct impact on the streets of Monstros.

Sensing danger, Billy reacted immediately, bringing the microphone up to his mouth.

"Heads up!" he screamed as loudly as he could.

The citizens looked up into the sky and scrambled for cover as an enormous boulder crashed down into the middle of the once-crowded street.

"That was close," Halifax said with a gulp.

The crowds in the streets of Monstros below were growing again, now starting to surround the resting boulder.

"Huh," Archebold said, scratching the top of his lumpy head with a chubby, clawed finger. "Wonder where that came from."

Billy felt himself growing angry. "Fly us over to the Frightening Forest," he said, returning the microphone to its place on the control panel. "Let's get a good look at this Zis-Boom-Bah and figure out how to kick his butt."

Archebold flew the Owlcopter over the sprawling city to the outskirts, and finally to the beginning of the Frightening Forest.

As Billy gazed out the windows of the copter at the thick vegetation, he could only wonder what lurked below to give the area such an ominous name.

"Why is it called the Frightening Forest?" he asked. "There are some real creepy critters living down there, I bet."

"Not really," Halifax said. "The name Scary Forest was already taken, and so was Terror Woods. Frightening Forest was what they finally settled on."

Archebold was nodding. "They almost called it The Place with a Lot of Trees, but they didn't want people to get it confused with some of the other places that had a lot of trees."

"I see," Billy said, certain that even if he continued to come to Monstros City for a thousand years, he'd never truly understand the place.

"Look down there," Archebold suddenly said, pointing toward a section of forest not too far from where the Abomination Mountain Range began.

A patch of woods was destroyed—trees knocked down, the ground overturned as if construction equipment had been used to clear it away.

"Just follow the destruction," Billy said, and Archebold did just that, tracing the path of devastation to a large body of emerald green water.

"That's Lake Lunatic," Halifax said, squeezing his shaggy head between the two front seats.

"What, was the name Big Body of Water already taken?"

Halifax and Archebold looked at him as though he had grown seven heads.

"Who would name a lake something like that?" the goblin asked.

"Yeah, that's just dumb," Halifax agreed. The troll then gasped, ducking down behind Billy's seat.

Billy was about to ask what was wrong when he saw it and immediately knew the answer.

"Oh my gosh!" he exclaimed as he stared down at the enormous monster squatting by the lake. "He's even bigger than I thought."

Billy watched, mesmerized, as Zis-Boom-Bah dipped one of his hands into Lake Lunatic and brought huge amounts of water to his thirsty mouth. Smacking his huge gorilla-like lips, he then reached out to some of the trees surrounding the lake, pulled them out by the roots and shoved them into his gigantic maw.

Even that high up, Billy could hear the nearly deafening sound of the monster's chewing.

Zis-Boom-Bah looked up in their direction.

"Not too close," Billy warned, not wanting to be mistaken for a flying snack.

Archebold steered the Owlcopter around Lake Lunatic to give them a good look from every angle.

"So, what are we gonna do?" Halifax asked, finding the bravery to peer out from between the seats again.

Billy didn't have a clue. If he had problems with the Sassafras Siblings and the Slovakian Rot-toothed Hopping Monkey Demons, what the heck was he going to do against a hundred-foot-tall monster?

"I don't know," he said, slowly shaking his head. And at that moment he didn't feel very much like a superhero. No, he felt like a scared little kid.

"But if you don't . . . who does?" Halifax asked.

Billy glanced at Archebold. The goblin was staring.

"Really," Billy said, starting to feel panicked. "I've got nothing."

"That isn't true," Archebold said as he flew the

Owlcopter around Zis-Boom-Bah again. "You're Owl-boy, and that's something special."

"But that monster is so much bigger than something special," Billy said, touching his goggles to activate the telescopic lenses so that he could get an even closer look at the threat.

"So much bigger."

Besides Zis-Boom-Bah's being ginormous and pretty scary-looking, Billy noticed something else. The monster's chewing had become slower; his eyelids looked heavier.

"I think he's getting sleepy," Billy said, and as if on cue, Zis-Boom-Bah yawned, giving them a most excellent view of his razor-sharp teeth and cavernous mouth.

"I think you're right," Archebold said. "So, how do you think we could use this to our advantage?"

Billy thought for a moment. "Well, if he's asleep, he isn't on the way to the city, and maybe that'll give us time to get back to the Roost and work on something that we could put into action before he wakes up."

Billy immediately felt better, the juices again flowing in his brain.

"I knew you'd come up with something," Halifax cheered, reaching over the seat to squeeze Billy's shoulder.

"No parties yet; this is just the first step," Billy

commented. "Let's wait until he drifts off, and then we'll see what we can come up with back at the Roost."

"Sounds like a plan," Archebold said, going around the back of the beast.

Zis-Boom-Bah was now sitting on the shore of Lake Lunatic, his enormous shoulders slumped, his breathing becoming slower.

"Won't be long now," Billy said as he watched the giant monster drift off to sleep.

Something flew by the cockpit of the Owlcopter with a hiss.

"What the heck?" Billy asked, watching as whatever it was crashed down on the shore of the lake and exploded in a ball of fire.

Zis-Boom-Bah was instantly awake, hopping to his reptilian feet, roaring at the sky as more of the fiery projectiles rained down with equally explosive results.

"Those are missiles!" Billy screamed. "Who the heck is firing missiles?"

"Look over there," Halifax said, practically in the front seat with them as he pointed.

Archebold steered the Owlcopter in that direction and Billy couldn't believe his eyes.

"Is that an army down there?" he asked.

There were green trucks parked in the Frightening Forest, soldiers carrying rifles jumping from the backs of the transports, ready for action. Billy saw tanks as well as rocket launchers getting into position for further attack.

"It's the Monstros City Defense Corps," Archebold said.

"What the heck do you need an army for?" Billy cried.

"We have quite a few parades and—"

The goblin's answer was cut short as another barrage of rockets was fired.

"Hold on!" Archebold screeched, moving the Owl-copter out of the path of the deadly projectiles.

The missiles just missed them, passing beneath the copter's belly on their way toward the angry monster.

"This isn't gonna be good," Billy said, suddenly feeling just a little bit psychic as the rockets struck the monster's chest in an explosion of orange flame and smoke.

Zis-Boom-Bah charged out of the roiling black smoke, angered by the attack. One of his huge hands shot out toward the Owlcopter despite Archebold's best efforts to get out of the way.

The copter was swatted aside like an annoying in-sect. As they spun out of control, the view of the forest below became much more up close and personal.

Rushing up to show them just how frightening it could be.

CHAPTER EIGHT

The full-blooming foliage of the trees acted as a kind of net as the Owlcopter dropped from the sky after being swatted like a fly by the hundred-foot-tall monster.

Billy and Archebold flopped around in the front seats, held in place by their seat belts, as Halifax bounced around the back of the copter, unrestrained and screaming like a nut.

The Owlcopter's weight brought them slowly down through the leaves, the bows of the trees moaning and snapping in protest as the disabled craft gradually made its way through the thick canopy to eventually hit the forest floor with a bone-jarring crash.

Billy remained perfectly still in his seat, waiting to see if they were finished falling.

"That was crazy," Archebold finally said, his eyes bugging out of his head.

They heard a moan from the back and turned to see Halifax crammed into the corner of the copter, looking like a tossed bag of laundry.

"You all right there, buddy?" Archebold asked.

The troll moaned again, slowly opening his eyes. "I think we need some more padding back here," he said with a groan. "My bumps have got bumps." Halifax slowly crawled to his feet, his bones popping and cracking as he flexed his fingers and wiggled his appendages. "Though nothing seems broken."

Still strapped in, Billy did the same. First he wiggled all his fingers, then his toes inside his boots. Everything seemed to be in working order.

"Can't believe we survived that in one piece," Archebold said, looking out the shattered window beside him. The goblin undid his safety belt and gave the door a push, the tiny pieces of glass tinkling down as it slowly swung open with a moan of bending metal.

Billy followed suit, brushing the diamond-like glass pieces from his costume as he emerged from the wreckage.

The craft trembled and groaned as Halifax struggled from the back, crawling over the seats, then falling from Billy's door to the ground.

"Land," he said as he dug his nails into the forest

floor and started kissing the dirt. "I never knew it could feel so good."

"All right, drama queen," Archebold said as he came around from inspecting the twisted wreckage, "put your Best Actress award away and see if there's a chance this thing can be fixed."

Halifax climbed to his feet. "I'll give you a chance for the Best Punch in the Coconut award, you little creep," the troll grumbled as he shook his fist at his friend.

"Lighten up, Mary," Archebold said, continuing to tease.

Billy took the opportunity to jump in, seeing that this was likely to go nowhere good.

"Guys," Billy said, standing between the feuding creatures. "Wrecked Owlcopter . . . giant monster . . . remember?"

"Sorry, Billy," Archebold said, straightening out his tuxedo jacket and wiping glittering glass fragments from his sleeve.

Halifax seemed sorry as well, doing as Archebold asked by checking out the Owlcopter.

"Not pretty," the troll said as he shook his shaggy head. "I don't see this thing getting off the ground any time soon."

Billy punched a gloved fist into his palm. "Nuts," he grumbled. "What're we gonna do?"

Before his friends could answer, they felt the ground begin to tremble and shake as during an earthquake.

If only it were something as simple as that, Billy thought.

Zis-Boom-Bah was on the move again, and it looked as if he was heading right for Monstros City.

"We've got to get to the city ahead of Zis-Boom-Bah," Billy announced. "Maybe those army guys who started this mess will give us a ride to—"

And as if on cue, the army guys of the Monstros City Defense Corps exploded from the woods, guns raised, their roaring vehicles pushing aside the thick vegetation as if it were nothing more than twigs.

"Here's your chance to ask them," Archebold said.

The army was made up of monsters of every species Billy could imagine, and some he couldn't. They were all dressed in dark green uniforms and wore helmets that looked like turtle shells.

"Put your hands up!" barked one of the soldiers, aiming down the length of his rifle with one of his four eyes.

Billy and his companions immediately did as they were told while the soldiers stalked closer.

"Who are you supposed to be?" a soldier with a head like a hard-boiled egg asked, sneering.

"Duh! What, have you been in a coma for the last few months?" Archebold asked. "He's Owlboy."

"The superhero Owlboy?" another of the soldiers

asked. This one resembled a salamander but with spiky orange hair that stuck out like quills from the sides of his helmet.

"No, the alligator wrestler Owlboy," Archebold said with disgust.

"There's an Owlboy who wrestles alligators?" asked Halifax.

Archebold gave the troll the evil eye. "Did you have to go to a special school to be this dumb?"

Billy thought he might have to separate the two again.

But then Hard-boiled-egg-head suddenly screamed, "Atten-hut!" and all the soldiers stood at attention.

Billy and the others found themselves doing the same as a short, squat figure jumped down from one of the military vehicles and pushed his way through the crowd of soldiers.

He was no taller than Billy and had a head like a bulldog's. On his jacket were row upon row of shiny medals, and across the front of his turtle-shell helmet were five stars. Billy believed that the bulldog guy had to be some sort of general.

"Who are these civilians?" the bulldog asked, his voice low and raw, a pink tongue snaking from his mouth over his protruding lower teeth to lick the white muzzle above his nose.

"They say the middle one is Owlboy, General Bludangutts," Egg-head told his commanding officer.

"Owlboy," the general snorted. "Didn't think we had one of them anymore."

Billy saw this as the opportunity he was looking for.

"I'm the new one, sir," Billy said, stepping forward.

The soldiers snapped to attention, aiming their rifles at him again.

"At ease, soldiers," Bludangutts ordered his men, and they promptly obeyed.

The general looked Billy up and down.

"Hurrumph," he snorted. "What are you doing here, Owlboy, and why are you interfering in a military operation?" the bulldog-faced officer finally asked, arms clasped behind his back.

"We didn't know we were interfering, sir," Billy said, attempting to explain. "We were trying to figure out how we could prevent Zis-Boom-Bah from reaching the city when you and your men started firing missiles and he knocked us out of the sky."

Bludangutts stepped in closer to Billy, his beady dog eyes locked on Billy's goggles. "Are you implying that we're responsible for your being knocked from the sky?" the bulldog asked.

His breath smelled like old sneakers stuffed with cheese. Billy backed up a few steps to avoid tipping over backward.

"Well, what I mean is . . . ," Billy began, waving a hand in front of his face to fan away the stink.

"What we mean to say is yes," Archebold said boldly. "Yes, if it wasn't for your stupid missiles, our copter wouldn't have crashed, and Zis-Boom-Bah would probably be sound asleep right now instead of stomping his way toward Monstros."

The general suddenly looked furious.

"Balderdash!" the bulldog screamed, stomping one of his booted feet on the ground. "If we hadn't been trying to avoid hitting you, our missiles would have been successful in taking the huge brute down."

Halifax started to laugh. "You don't actually expect us to believe that, do you?" the troll asked, still chuckling.

"Every word," Bludangutts growled.

"Just checking," Halifax answered sheepishly, quickly stepping back behind Billy.

"But we've lost the element of surprise," the bulldog growled. "The brute will be expecting them now." Bludangutts began to pace in a circle around Billy, Archebold and Halifax. "We have to come up with something new, if we're going to take him out."

Billy turned to face the general. "If you would give me a little time, I'm sure I can come up with a way to—"

"You?" Bludangutts asked while his soldiers started to chuckle as if the idea were totally absurd. "What is a lone superhero going to do against one hundred feet of gut-crunching, city-stomping terror?"

Billy thought for a moment, hoping that an answer would come to him.

"Right this second I've got nothing," he admitted honestly. "But with a little time . . ."

"A little time we don't have, civilian," Bludangutts roared.

Another figure emerged to join them from the midst of the military vehicles. It was a large praying mantis who wore a white lab coat and had a black toupee on top of his triangular head.

What is it with all these monsters and toupees? Billy thought before paying attention to what the mantis was saying.

"Did I hear somebody say something about needing a deadly weapon?" the mantis asked, rubbing his hooked appendages together excitedly.

"I did, at that, Professor," Bludangutts answered.

"Who are you supposed to be?" Archebold asked.

"I am Professor Carapace," the mantis said with a bow, "the Monstros City military's weapons specialist. And I believe I have just the thing to destroy our enemy."

The insect turned his bulbous eyes toward Bludangutts, completely ignoring Billy and his pals.

"Go on, Professor. I'm listening," the bulldog said.

"Yeah, so am I," Archebold said.

"And me too," Billy said.

"The more, the merrier," Halifax said, and laughed nervously.

"Conventional weaponry will most assuredly fail when we are dealing with a threat as large as this one," the bug calmly explained. "A weapon of equal ferocity must be utilized."

"And if I'm not mistaken, you have such a weapon, Professor?" Bludangutts asked.

"I most certainly do," the insect said, his buzzing voice getting higher as he became more excited. "And I've been waiting a very long time to try it out."

They all waited while Professor Carapace paused as if for dramatic effect.

"I suggest we detonate the O.M.G. device," the mantis said, his head bobbing up and down as he rubbed his two sharp, buggy-looking front arms together.

"Are you out of your mind?" Archebold screeched. "Pinch me; I've got to be having a nightmare!"

Bludangutts ignored the goblin's outburst, his paw-like hand stroking the loose skin beneath his chin.

"An excellent suggestion," the general said. "I've been itching to try out the O.M.G. on something for a long time."

"Is this the O.M.G. that I think it is?" Halifax asked.

Archebold nodded furiously. "It's exactly the O.M.G. you think it is," he said, his voice sounding frantic.

"Catch me; I feel faint," Halifax said as his body went limp and he fell to their feet.

"I told you to catch me," the troll growled, looking up at them from the ground.

"Whoa!" Billy suddenly yelled, holding out his arms. "Wait just a minute. Would somebody mind explaining to me what this O.M.G. device is?"

"It's the deadliest weapon ever created in Monstros City," Archebold said. "So dangerous that most of the scientists in the city think it should never be used. Sure, it would likely destroy Zis-Boom-Bah, but it would also probably destroy all of Monstros City in the process."

Billy was stunned, having never imagined that the city of monsters could have a weapon of such power, but then again, he never imagined that they would have an army, either.

"Why do they call it that?" Billy asked, his curiosity getting the better of him. "Why do they call it the O.M.G. device?"

The goblin looked scared as he recalled the explanation.

"They called it that because when they first created that device, it was a much smaller version, and they tested it out in the Jugular Jungle."

"But I've never heard of the Jugular Jungle," Billy said.

"Exactly," Archebold said with foreboding in his voice. "It isn't there anymore."

Billy gulped loudly.

"The letters OMG stand for what all the scientists said when they saw how deadly it was," the goblin went on.

Billy started to think about what the three letters could stand for before Archebold finally filled in the blanks.

"*Oh my gosh* is what they said when they saw what the bomb could do. Oh. My. Gosh."

"So I'm guessing that using this O.M.G. device is a very bad idea," Billy said.

"And you would be oh so correct," Archebold agreed as Halifax nodded wildly beside him.

"My family had some friends who worked on that project, and when they were done, they never built or fixed anything ever again," Halifax said. "And that's very sad for a troll. They might as well be dead."

"We've gotta stop this," Billy said. As protector of Monstros, he couldn't let anybody do anything that could harm the city.

He stepped forward with as much authority as he could muster. Bludangutts and Carapace watched him with suspicious eyes.

"What if we could stop Zis-Boom-Bah without the O.M.G.?" Billy suggested.

The insect laughed. It was a high-pitched sound that made the insides of Billy's ears itch.

"What would you suggest?" Professor Carapace asked.

Billy had to be honest, and hoped that it might gain him their trust.

"I don't have that information just yet, but I can't imagine that it'll take me all that long."

"We don't have that kind of time, hero," Bludangutts barked. "The great beast is on the move right now. Every second we waste, the threat gets that much closer to our major metropolitan area, and I'm not going to allow that to happen."

The bulldog quickly spun around and headed back toward his military vehicle. Professor Carapace ran to catch up.

"Wait!" Billy yelled.

General Bludangutts stopped and slowly started to turn. It was obvious that he wasn't used to being given commands.

"I don't think you understand who you're talking to," Billy said, hooking a thumb at his chest. "I'm Owlboy. And this is just as much my city to protect as it is yours."

Bludangutts stalked quickly toward him, his hanging jowls quivering with anger. Billy held his ground, letting the dog creature get in his face.

"I've got a plan, hero," the bulldog growled. "What've you got?"

Billy did his best to keep calm. Archebold and Halifax had come to stand beside him.

"Give me a little bit of time to come up with something," Billy said. "That's all I'm asking."

The general spun around with a snort, hands clasped behind his back.

"Personally, I've always felt the whole Owlboy thing was a bit overrated," Bludangutts said. "But I like your spunk, hero." The bulldog-faced creature looked at the clunky watch on his sleeve. "I'll give you two hours— no more, no less—but when it's time to use the device, nothing you say is going to stop me."

Billy breathed a heavy sigh as the general stomped off with his men.

"Oh man," he said. "I didn't think that was going to work."

"It worked, all right," Archebold agreed. "But now we've got to figure out what we're going to do."

"I need some brain food," Halifax said, and he reached into the front pocket of his overalls and removed a fish. The troll took a huge bite of the snack and started to chew.

Billy and Archebold just stared.

"Want a bite?" he asked, holding out the fish.

Billy's brain was suddenly hit by the beginning of an idea. "Wait a sec," he said. "Zis-Boom-Bah was really slowed down while he was eating by the lake. In fact, he was almost asleep."

"Yeah," Archebold said eagerly. "Go on."

"Well, what if we gave him something more delicious than trees to eat? I bet that would slow him down big-time and give us even more time to come up with a way to keep him out of Monstros."

"What would we give him?" Halifax asked, his mouth filled with brain food.

"Snacks," Billy said, knowing in his gut that he was on to something. "Lots and lots of delicious snacks."

"Excellent idea," Archebold said, his eyes twinkling with excitement. But then Billy watched as the goblin's expression started to change.

"What's wrong?" Billy asked.

"Zis-Boom-Bah is one pretty big dude," Archebold stated. "How do we get that many snacks into his general vicinity?"

Billy stroked his chin with a gloved hand. "We need to get out of here first. I'm sure there's something back at the Roost we can use," he said, flexing the muscles of his brain. "But currently we're without transportation, unless . . ."

They both looked at Halifax, who was finishing up

his snack. The tail of the fish was just disappearing into his wide mouth.

"What?" Halifax asked.

"Well, you say you can fix anything, right?" Billy said to the troll.

"Yeah, I have been known to say that," Halifax agreed.

"Could you fix the Owlcopter?"

The troll walked through the woods to the wreckage of their craft. Billy and Archebold followed.

"Nope," the troll said, shaking his head. "Not a chance of repairing that."

Billy and Archebold sighed. If they couldn't get out of the Frightening Forest and back to the city right away, their time to come up with a plan would be used up.

"Unless . . . ," Halifax said, reaching into his front overall pocket and coming up this time with a really big wrench. He approached the copter as Billy and Archebold watched.

"This might take me a while," the troll said, disappearing inside the craft, where a symphony of banging began.

Billy and Archebold wandered away from the wreckage. Less than a minute later, they heard Halifax call out.

They both turned as the troll came through the bushes, pushing an entirely new vehicle made from parts salvaged from the Owlcopter. The new device had a single seat, with a powerful-looking engine attached to spin the Owlcopter's former rotor blades.

"What the heck is that?" Archebold asked.

"I could only make it a one-seater," Halifax explained, scratching his furry head. "But I managed to salvage enough to whip up something else."

The troll disappeared through the bushes again and returned almost instantly with something that looked like a motorized unicycle.

"Wow," Billy said, looking more closely at the tiny copter, then at the new, single-wheeled mode of conveyance. "This is really nuts. How did you manage all this?"

The troll shrugged. "Would've been quicker, but I ran out of parts." He leaned in close to them, cupping a hand to his mouth, and whispered, "Had to borrow some odds and ends from the army's trucks."

They all looked toward the Monstros City Defense Corps' camp.

"What they don't know won't hurt 'em," Archebold said with a wink.

Billy squatted down on his haunches, picking up a pointed stick. "Okay, here's the plan," he said, drawing two figures in the dirt.

"Who're they supposed to be?" Halifax asked. "Are those supposed to be me and Archebold? Which one is me? If you ask me, none of them are capturing the subtle differences in our—"

Archebold smacked the troll on the top of his head.

"Oww!" Halifax bellowed.

"Thank you," Billy said to Archebold.

"Don't mention it," the goblin replied. "Proceed."

Billy drew a circle around the two figures. "You guys are going to get back to Monstros as quick as you can and get your hands on as many snacks are you're able to. You've seen how big Zis-Boom-Bah is; we're gonna need a lot of snacks."

Archebold stroked his chin in thought. "I think I know just the place where we can get our hands on the snacks we need."

"And back at the garage I've got just the thing to transport them to Zis-Boom-Bah," Halifax piped up.

"Excellent," Billy said, now drawing himself in the dirt. "I'm going back to the Roost to see what I can come up with to put a stop to the threat of Zis-Boom-Bah for good."

They all stood up, ready to go.

"Remember, Bludangutts has only given us two hours before he decides to use the O.M.G.," Billy said. "We've got to make every second count."

They headed toward the new vehicles Halifax had created.

"You take the mini-chopper," Halifax said to Billy. "Pedal with your feet here, and steer with this," the troll explained, pointing out the new helicopter's controls.

"What about you guys?" Billy asked as he sat down on the craft and fastened his seat belt. Snapped in, he pointed to the unicycle. "That looks like it was only built for one."

The troll chuckled as he started to climb onto the seat. "Looks can be deceiving," he said. He flicked a switch on the side of his seat, and the engine roared to life. Suddenly the one-wheeled cycle was perfectly balanced, rocking slightly from side to side.

"Hop on," he told Archebold, pointing to his shoulders.

"Why do I get the feeling that I'm going to regret this?" Archebold asked, using the vehicle's single wheel to climb up onto Halifax and throwing his stubby legs over the troll's shoulders.

"Regrets are for wimps," Halifax said, flicking another switch on the side of the seat, sending the unicycle roaring forward.

"Good luck, Billy!" Halifax yelled as he rode off into the woods, navigating the trees, rocks and bushes with incredible speed.

"See ya later!" Archebold squealed, holding on to Halifax's hair for dear life. "I hope!"

And they were gone in a flash.

"My turn," Billy muttered beneath his breath, planting his feet firmly on the rubber footrests and starting to pedal. The twin blades above his head began to turn slowly, the engine at his back humming to life.

Within seconds he had lifted off, flying above the Frightening Forest, on the most important mission of his career as the superhero protector of Monstros City.

CHAPTER NINE

Billy pedaled like crazy to keep the propellers spinning as he soared above the Frightening Forest. By moving the hand control, he was able to steer the new craft forward and backward, left and right.

That Halifax is something, he thought, marveling at how quickly the troll had managed to throw the mini-chopper together. He recalled how long it had taken him to build his first time machine, and in the end, that hadn't even worked.

Gazing down from his seat at the forest below, he could see the path of destruction left by Zis-Boom-Bah and, a little bit farther on, the big beast himself.

Pushing down on the control stick, Billy directed the craft forward, toward the enormous monster.

Zis-Boom-Bah seemed to have stopped. He appeared to be clearing an area of vegetation, ripping the huge trees up by the roots and tossing them aside. He didn't seem to be hungry anymore, but he did seem to be up to something.

Billy kept a safe distance from the strange creature, hovering above his head like a bird in the sky.

Zis-Boom-Bah kicked at the ground with his dinosaur feet, overturning the dirt.

What the heck is he doing? Billy wondered, flying a wide circle around the giant monster.

Finished with the dirt, Zis-Boom-Bah left momentarily and returned, his arms filled with a few of what to Billy were gigantic boulders but to the huge animal were similar to good-sized cantaloupes.

Curiously, Billy watched as the monster threw the boulders on the ground, dropped to his knees and arranged the huge rocks in a pile.

Then the monstrous force of nature flopped down on his back and rested his big monkey head atop the rocks, using them as a pillow.

"He's taking a nap!" Billy exclaimed gleefully. He knew that that bought him some time. The big beast folded his hands across his chest and closed his eyes. Within seconds, he started to snore.

Not knowing how long this good fortune might last, Billy decided that he'd better get out of there.

He pedaled back to the Roost as fast as he was able to.

"It's right over there," Archebold cried over the rumbling motor of the unicycle, still riding on Halifax's shoulders, holding on to two big handfuls of the troll's hair.

Halifax leaned his weight to one side, steering the single-wheeled vehicle around the corner and into the parking lot of Sammy's House of Snacks.

The unicycle came to a halt in front of the warehouse-sized store. Archebold leaped down to the ground, grateful that he'd made the trip in one piece. He realized he was still holding a brown tuft of troll hair in each of his tiny fat-fingered hands.

Archebold smiled nervously as he caught Halifax staring at him, the troll rubbing the top of his head where he'd once had more hair.

"You want this back?" Archebold asked with nervous chuckle. "It's very nice, by the way," he said, rubbing the hair against his cheek. "Very soft."

"You can keep it," Halifax growled. "Hopefully it'll grow back."

"That's the spirit," Archebold said as he flung the two clumps of hair over his shoulder and wiped his hands on the front of his pants. "Let's go see what kind of deal we can make with Sammy for a coupla tons of snacks." They walked up to the automatic doors, which slid open with a serpentlike hiss.

The warehouse was strangely empty.

Odd, Archebold thought. Sammy's was the main distributor of snacks of all kinds to all the major food outlets in Monstros City. *The place should be much busier than this.*

"Hello?" Archebold called out. His voice echoed slightly.

They looked around for anybody who could help them, but found no one. The warehouse was filled with boxes of every conceivable size and shape, and all Archebold had to do was close his eyes and breathe deeply to allow the delectable aroma of some of the city's finest snack products wash over him. Cockroach cakes, bloodberry pies, Captain Tasty's Fungus Fondue, and honey-roasted barbecued scabs. Archebold's mouth had begun to water, and he was doing everything in his power to keep from drooling. He had to remind himself that they were on an important mission.

"Do you hear that?" Halifax asked.

"Hear what?" the goblin asked, cupping one of his unusually large ears and listening very carefully. "I don't hear any—"

And then he heard it: it sounded like the muttering of a voice and the wrinkling of paper.

"I think it's coming from down there," Halifax said, pointing toward the back of the building.

They headed in that direction.

"Hello, hello!" Archebold called again as they went around a corner of stacked boxes. The goblin could smell that they were filled with Sweet and Sour Berry Bugs, one of his personal favorites.

A monster buzzed on dragonfly-type wings at the back of the aisle. He was long and thin, his multiple arms holding multiple computer printouts that he dropped to the floor right after he read them.

"I'm ruined . . . *ruined!*" the insectoid buzzed in panic.

"Is that him?" Halifax asked.

Archebold nodded, moving down the aisle. "Think so. How's tricks, Sammy?" he asked, trying to sound cooler than he was. He didn't want to seem desperate in front of the store owner; the insect could smell desperate like a wereweasel could smell chili fries.

The insect spun around in the air, a look of absolute hopelessness in his bulbous eyes. He was wearing a bright red bow tie and a spiffy green leisure suit. Archebold made a mental note to ask him where he bought his clothes once they got through with this giant-monster business.

"I'm ruined," he buzzed. "Ruined, I say."

"What's wrong?" Archebold asked.

"What's wrong?" Sammy repeated. "You have to ask what's wrong?" He flung out his four arms, gesturing to the many stacked pallets, boxes and shelves, all filled with product. "This is what's wrong."

Archebold and Halifax looked around.

"Looks okay to me," Halifax said, licking his lips.

"Me too," Archebold agreed. "Lots and lots of snacks!"

"Exactly!" Sammy screeched. "Lots and lots of snacks . . . not a shelf, not a pallet that isn't stacked high with delectable goodness. Snacks as far as the eye can see!"

"This is a good thing, right?" Archebold asked.

"It's a terrible thing!" Sammy screamed, again looking around the packed warehouse. "These shelves and pallets should be empty, the snacks on the way to countless stores throughout our fair city of Monstros, but here they sit . . . rotting."

The insectoid looked up suddenly.

"Have you ever smelled rotting Squid MacNuggets? It's not pleasant."

"So why . . . ?" Archebold began.

"I'll tell you why! Because of this giant beastie, this *Zis-Boom-Bah*. People are afraid to leave their homes!

Businesses are closed up tighter than a blood bank on Dracula's birthday."

"Now, that's tight," Halifax agreed, nodding.

"And here they sit," Sammy went on. "Tons and tons of snacks with nobody to eat them."

The insectoid's wings suddenly stopped fluttering and he slumped to the ground, defeated.

"What am I gonna do with all these wasted snacks? I'm ruined—ruined, I say!"

Archebold couldn't help smiling as he reached out and put a comforting arm around Sammy's waist.

"Sammy," the goblin said, "I think we're the answer to your prayers."

The Monarch turned the knob of his eye-shaped viewing monitor, tuning in to the special news alert that was being broadcast on all Monstros City's stations . . . except for channel forty-nine. It was still playing a game show, *Bowling for Gizzards*.

Nothing gets between a Monstros City citizen and his Bowling for Gizzards, the Monarch thought.

Monstros was in a panic, and within the darkness of his hood, the overlord of criminal activity in the city of monsters smiled. It was all that he had hoped for and more.

A buzzer announced that he had company, and he pushed a button on a nearby control panel to open the doors to his lab.

"Enter," the criminal mastermind demanded, continuing to watch the news broadcast. The Monarch was even pleased to hear that the giant-monster attack had managed to foul up snack distribution to the city.

Oh, I've outdone myself on this one, the Monarch thought, congratulating himself with an evil chuckle.

The Monarch realized that he was no longer alone and, though it was difficult, turned his chair slowly away from the monitor displaying the most devastating example of his evil abilities. He gazed at his guests.

Klot and Mukus looked as though they had fallen down a mountain.

"What on earth has happened to you two?" the Monarch asked, stunned by their disheveled appearance.

"We fell down the mountain," Klot said, swaying where he stood as Mukus nodded in agreement beside him.

The heavy clothing they had worn on their mission to awaken the great beast Zis-Boom-Bah in Mount Terror was tattered and torn, stained with dirt and mud.

"How dare you appear before your lord and master in such a state," the Monarch snarled.

"Please forgive us, oh mighty Monarch," Mukus said. "But after we fell down the mountain, we were covered up in an avalanche and had to dig ourselves out."

"Hrrrumph," the crime master grumbled. "I remember a time when lackeys made it a point to clean up and dress in their finest attire when standing before their superiors."

"We would have preferred to stop and clean up—and visit the emergency room—before standing before you, great one, but we wanted to get back here as quickly as possible to inform you of our success."

The Monarch turned his chair partially around so that he could see the eye-shaped monitor.

"Don't you mean *my* success?" he asked.

He watched as Klot and Mukus made eye contact with each other.

"Of course *your* success," Mukus said with a grin, a puddle of slime forming at his feet. "We wouldn't think of taking away from your accomplishments, oh mighty master of the underworld."

"We are just hollow vessels carrying your liquidy criminal genius," Klot added, bowing to his master.

The Monarch was about to agree with them when his attention was snared by the appearance of a reporter on the monitor. She was looking very serious, her one eye extremely bloodshot, as if she had been crying.

He reached out and turned up the volume.

"Reports are coming in that the fate of our fair city's greatest hero, Owlboy, is unknown. The Owlcopter was completely destroyed when it was knocked from the sky in a terrifying attack by the monster known as Zis-Boom-Bah."

The reporter paused to dab at her tearing single orb with a handkerchief.

"To repeat our sad story: the hero of Monstros City—Owlboy—may have been killed in a horrible attack. . . ."

The Monarch let out an ear-piercing cry, suddenly standing up from his chair, hands in the air. He slowly turned toward his lackeys, who now clung together in fear at his outburst.

And for the first time in many, many years, the criminal mastermind began to laugh.

CHAPTER TEN

Billy found a place to land his mini-Owlcopter in the giant branches of the gigantic tree that housed the Roost.

His leg muscles were burning from pedaling, and he hoped that he wouldn't get a cramp as he ran down the length of a branch toward a door that would bring him into the garage.

There isn't any time for cramps, he thought as he threw open the door and stepped into the vehicle storage hangar. He looked at his surroundings, at the various Owl-inspired vehicles, trying to find something to stop Zis-Boom-Bah from stomping Monstros into crumbs.

"If only we had an interplanetary rocket craft in here," he said, walking around the Owl-golf-cart and almost tripping over the Owl-tricycle. In his mind he pictured a huge rocket with an even huger capsule on top—a capsule big enough to hold Zis-Boom-Bah.

But that was crazy; it would be too big for the storage hangar. And even if that was the idea he was going to go with, how much time would it take to build something like that?

The kind of time he just didn't have. He pulled down the sleeve of his glove and looked at the Owlwatch on his wrist. The time given to him was flying as fast as summer vacation in August. He needed to move—and quickly.

Billy descended in the elevator, hoping to grab a drink and a little something to nibble on from the snack room. Snacking helped him think, and if there was one thing he should be doing now, it was thinking.

His mind was wild with activity, like a hamster on a sugar high running round and round on its wheel.

The doors slid open and he charged from the elevator toward the snack room. Maybe there would be some of those little bloodberry pies he loved so much.

They tasted like chicken, but in a delicious fruity, cakey sort of way.

Billy stopped short, looking around. He didn't see the door to the snack room anywhere and realized that he must've gotten off on the wrong floor.

"Crap," he said beneath his breath, running back toward the elevators just as the heavy metal doors slid shut.

"Double crap on a piece of bread," he said, stomping his foot and pounding one of his gloved fists against the closed door. He jabbed the return button with a finger and leaned back, waiting for the elevator to arrive.

"Don't think I've ever been on this floor before," he muttered, leaving his place to check out the labels on the doors.

Most of them just said "storage," but there was one that intrigued him.

"Archives," Billy said as he read the sign hanging in the center of the yellow door. "Hmmmmmmmmmm."

He reached for the owl-head-shaped doorknob and turned it. The door swung open to reveal a room that at first glance seemed to be filled only with darkness.

Billy reached inside to let his hand fish around for a light switch.

"Gotcha!" he said, finding what he was looking for and flooding the room with light.

"WOWZA!" Billy exclaimed as he slowly entered. The archives room was filled with shelves—row upon row of shelves—and on those shelves was every kind of reading material available: scrolls, stone tablets, newspapers, books and, yes—his favorite—comic books.

"Would you look at all this stuff!" he said, reaching out to pick up one of the rolled scrolls from the shelf. He carefully unfurled the ancient document and saw that it was written in a foreign language he couldn't read, but there were some wonky drawings here and there, and from the artwork, he guessed it was telling about a really old version of Owlboy kicking butt on some nasty old-time villain.

This Owlboy was *particularly* interesting, because the drawings showed him wearing only bikini briefs, a mask and a cape made from lots of feathers.

"Nice," Billy said with a roll of his eyes, placing the scroll back on the shelf where he'd found it.

He figured that this was where they kept the printed records of the different Owlboys' adventures throughout the ages. The comic books were really interesting, and he guessed that they were printed by a publisher in Monstros, because they were not at all like the ones he had in his own collection back home.

"Awesome," he said in a whisper, snatching up an issue from a dusty stack and immediately starting to flip through it.

He would love to have some of these but wasn't sure if they would survive the journey. Things made in Monstros were pretty much supposed to stay in Monstros. Billy imagined the Monstros comics turning to dust in his hands, or maybe even bursting into flames, as they left the mausoleum.

Standing in the archives room, Billy had the beginning of a brainstorm.

"If these are the records of all the Owlboy adventures throughout time, there's got to be something in here that can help me out with the Zis-Boom-Bah problem," he said to himself. "All I have to do is read through it all."

He glanced at his watch and felt the grip of terror in the pit of his belly. It was even later than he'd expected. There was so much to read and so little time, but he had to at least give it a try.

Stroking his chin, Billy forced his brain cells to work, and he could have sworn he smelled burning plastic. He decided to read first the Owlboy comics published by Ghastly Comics, right there in Monstros.

The earliest issues were painted on heavy pieces of rock, with drawings that looked like they were done by a first-grader with a dull crayon, but there was still something incredibly cool about the simple stories of Monstros' first Owlboy.

After the stone tablets, the comics seemed to be painted on something that looked like it might be animal skin. There weren't many of those, and before he knew it, he was moving on to stories printed on what appeared to be paper.

Billy read as fast as he could, zipping through the amazing adventures of Owlboys from different time periods, all the while searching—hoping—for anything that could help him with his current predicament.

The comics were wicked entertaining, but they were pretty much the same thing over and over again: Owlboy discovered something wrong and then did his best to make it right. It was all very cool, especially seeing how the artists from Monstros drew the different versions of Owlboy, but it wasn't giving him anything he didn't already know.

Owlboy always triumphed over evil, which was all well and good, but it didn't help him with Monstros' current situation.

Billy was tempted to look at his watch again, but resisted. He knew he was running out of time; he didn't need his watch to tell him that. Instead, he dove into another box of the old comic books, mostly just flipping through the pictures now, trying to find something that resembled Zis-Boom-Bah.

He finished in record time but still didn't have what he needed. Frustrated, he tossed the box aside and was about to grab a stack of newspapers featuring front-page Owlboy headlines when, from the corner of his eye, he saw something else.

It was high on a shelf across the room: some colorful paper poking out from the top of a box. Billy played with the lenses on his goggles and used the telescopic feature to zoom in on the box. More comics.

But he had a good feeling about this box. (Or was it wishful thinking?) Carefully, he climbed onto a stack of boxes and extended his arms. His fingers just brushed the sides of his prize. The stack swayed a bit beneath him and he almost lost his balance, but he managed to steady himself by holding on to the shelf for a moment.

Billy looked up at the box again, took a deep breath and stood on tiptoe. The stack of boxes beneath him began to sway like a skyscraper during an earthquake, but he wasn't about to give up. He grabbed hold of the front corners of the mystery box and gave it a good yank.

The box moved toward him just as the world—well, not the world really, but the cardboard boxes beneath his boots—suddenly slid away from him.

It was over in seconds. The prized box flew out of his hands and he tumbled to the floor, whacking his noggin on the corner of a shelf.

For a moment, Billy just lay on the floor among the old newspapers, scrolls and crumpled and collapsed cardboard boxes as the entire universe swirled before his eyes.

Slowly, he began to crawl up from beneath the wreckage, his head feeling as though it were in a washing machine on the spin cycle. And then he gasped.

Billy was no longer alone.

The various Owlboys from all the ages were standing before him in their most heroic poses. He shook his head and looked again. They were still there.

"Hey, guys." He shrugged, giving them a careful wave. "How's it going?"

They seemed to relax a bit, crossing their arms as they looked at him.

"I'm an Owlboy too," he said with a dopey smile, plucking at the front of his costume. He started toward them and lost his balance, his head still spinning.

He had an idea. Crazy as it might be, what did he have to lose?

"Hey, since you're here and all, and probably figments of my imagination, I was wondering if any of you could give me some pointers on how to handle this Zis-Boom-Bah predicament."

The primitive Owlboy, in his feathered cape and tighty-whiteys, screamed something in his crazy language, pointed at the ceiling and faded away.

"Thanks," Billy replied, not having a clue what he'd just said.

The other Owlboys started yelling as well, their words all jumbled together, and after their proclamations, they too faded away.

"The forces of evil shall feel the sting of my beak!"

"The talons of the owl tingle with the promise of vanquishing evil."

"Hooooot! Hooooooot! Hoooooooooooooooooooot!"

Billy listened to each and every one, even the hooter, looking for a nugget that he could grab hold of, polish and turn into a way to defeat the enormous threat to the safety of the city of monsters.

He hadn't heard anything helpful yet, but he still had hope.

"Always brush your teeth, fangs and beak," said one of the Owlboys, wearing a particularly shiny suit of armor, before fading away with a metallic clatter.

"Interesting," Billy commented with a nod. "Not very helpful, but interesting."

"Pluck the weed of villainy before it grows," said another as he wrapped himself up in his cape, spinning like a twister before disappearing.

There was one Owlboy remaining, and Billy thought that he just might fade away like the others before giving him his final words of wisdom.

"Wait!" Billy called out to the last of the ghostly figures. "Don't you have anything to say to me? Anything at all?"

This version of Owlboy stroked his powerful-looking square chin and seemed to be deep in thought when suddenly he smiled. Billy could've sworn he saw the Owlboy's eyes twinkle behind the older and much larger version of his goggles as he raised a finger in the air to make his point.

"Know your enemies," he stated, wagging his finger. "Know them well enough to turn their own dastardliness against them."

Billy listened, expecting more, but the last of the old Owlboys was fading away.

"That's all you've got?" he called. "Nothing else?"

Billy rubbed the tender spot on his head. At least the dizziness was gone. The words of the last Owlboy, though, remained fresh in his mind.

Know your enemies. Know them well enough to turn their own dastardliness against them.

Billy stopped rubbing his head as an idea slowly began to form.

"Turn their own dastardliness against them," he repeated, a smile spreading across his face. "Why didn't I think of that?"

Billy exited the elevator on the floor of the observation room and heard Archebold and Halifax chattering wildly.

He hurried down the hall and entered the monitoring center just as the two creatures were thumping their chests together in a display of victory.

Archebold was tossed back by Halifax's more power-ful efforts and fell to the floor.

"What the heck are you two doing?" Billy asked. His run-in with the Owlboys in the archives, as successful as it had been, had cost him precious time and he knew there wasn't much left.

The goblin was laughing as he got up. "We knocked this one out of the park, Billy."

"A home run!" Halifax said, raising his hand for Archebold to give him a high five.

"What happened?" Billy asked, his curiosity piqued. "What did you do?"

"We hit the snack jackpot," Archebold said, slap-ping the palm of his four-fingered hand into Halifax's with a loud smack.

"All right. Seeing as I don't speak crazy person, could you maybe explain to me what you're talking about?"

"Those snacks you needed?" Archebold asked. "We went into Sammy's Snacks, showed 'em we meant busi-ness and got one sweet deal of a discount on all the snacks we could need and then some."

"That's awesome," Billy agreed, raising his own hand to join in on the high-five palooza.

"Of course, we got the deal because all the snacks were gonna go rotten in a day or so anyway because all the stores are closed because of Zis-Boom-Bah coming to destroy Monstros City and stuff," Halifax added.

"Details, details," the goblin said, waving his hand. "We still got the snacks at a steal."

"Exactly," Billy said. "Good job, guys."

They all paused, staring at each other and smiling and basking in their victory.

"So, how'd you do, Billy?" Archebold asked. "Come up with anything that we can use to defeat the monster once and for all?"

"Yeah, did you put that super-owl brain of yours to work?" Halifax asked, eager to hear.

Billy could barely contain his excitement. "I think I have," he said. "I was up in the archives room and these ghosts—"

"Ghosts!" Archebold exclaimed. "You saw ghosts . . . real ghosts?"

"Yeah, I think they were ghosts—of past Owlboys—but they were saying—"

"What're we gonna do?" Halifax suddenly screamed, his voice trembling with fear. "First Zis-Boom-Bah and now ghosts! I think I'm gonna have a nervous breakdown."

The troll started to sway on his feet as if about to pass out.

"Hold it together, pal," Archebold said. "The kid

said that they were ghosts of past Owlboys. Maybe they're not too scary."

Billy didn't know what to think. Here he was, standing in a room with a goblin and a troll, in a giant tree growing up from the center of a creepy forest, in a city inhabited by monsters.

And they were afraid of ghosts.

"I don't know if they were even real ghosts. They might've just been figments of my imagination and stuff because I hit my head pretty good on a shelf, but anyway—"

"So there's a chance that they weren't real ghosts?" Halifax asked carefully.

"Yes," Billy agreed, trying to make the troll feel better. "It could've just been head trauma, but that doesn't change the fact that they gave me some information I think might help us defeat Zis-Boom-Bah."

He waited for their reaction.

"I don't know about you, but I'm feeling better," Archebold said, wiping sweat from his wrinkled brow. "Ghosts are the last thing I need to be dealing with, if you know what I mean."

Halifax seemed relieved as well.

"These kids and their overactive imaginations," the troll said with a chuckle, pointing at Billy. "Ghosts. What will they think of next?"

The troll and the goblin started to laugh and Billy thought he might lose it.

"Forget the ghosts!" Billy screamed, stomping one of his feet. "Did either of you hear what I just said about possibly having the answer to how to stop Zis-Boom-Bah from reaching Monstros and destroying it?"

"Does it have anything to do with ghosts?" Halifax asked.

"No. It does not have anything to do with ghosts," Billy growled, grinding his teeth together. If steam could have shot from his ears, it would have.

"Then let's hear it," Archebold said, giving Billy's shoulder a smack. "We're wasting valuable time."

For a quick minute, Billy wished that Zis-Boom-Bah was there then, his huge foot dropping down from the ceiling to squash Billy's two pain-in-the-neck friends, but he managed to pull himself together and get control of his temper.

"The ghosts said—"

Halifax gasped, jamming his knuckles into his mouth with fright.

"Sorry. The figments of my imagination said some pretty wild things, mostly stuff about fighting and vanquishing evil."

Halifax seemed to relax, and both he and Archebold were now listening.

"But it was the last Owlboy figment that really gave me what I was looking for."

"What did it say, Billy?" Archebold asked excitedly.

Billy paused for dramatic effect.

"He said that I should know my enemies, and use their own dastardliness against them."

Billy waited for what he was sure would be an overwhelming reaction.

The two creatures just stared blankly.

"Get it?" Billy asked. "I'm to use a villain's own dastardliness against him."

Archebold and Halifax looked at each other, their expressions still blank, and turned the empty gazes back to him.

"Guess this is gonna take a bit more work," Billy said. "You see, what I think the ghost . . . What the figment of my imagination was trying to say was that I should use my enemies' *strengths* against them."

He waited, searching for something—any sign that this was sinking in. Billy half expected to see a plastic Christmas village with snow falling on it while looking into Halifax's blank stare.

"So I started to think about all the different Owlboy cases I read about, and how those Owlboys defeated their foes, which led me to start thinking about the villains I've fought, and *then* it hit me."

"A ghost didn't hit you, did it?" Halifax asked, looking frightened again.

"Will you stop with the ghosts!" Billy yelled. "When I started thinking of the villains I've fought and their strengths, I immediately thought of Dr. Bug. And what made Dr. Bug a formidable foe?" Billy asked them, not really expecting any answers.

"His shrink gun." Billy answered his own question. "And from there it all fell into place. I'm going down to the Monstros City Police Headquarters to ask to borrow Dr. Bug's shrink gun and use it to shrink Zis-Boom-Bah down to a more manageable size."

Billy crossed his arms, feeling a tad exhausted from laying out his plans.

"So, what do you think of that?"

Archebold looked at Halifax and then back at Billy.

"You're a genius!" the goblin shrieked. "That's a great plan that only a true Owlboy could've thought up, sir." Archebold patted Billy on the back. "And while you're doing that, Halifax and I are going to inflate the Owlblimp and fly it over to—"

"We have a blimp?" Billy interrupted.

"Of course we do," Archebold answered. "We're going to take the Owlblimp over to Sammy's Snacks and pick up our load o' snacks and we'll meet you at . . ."

Halifax had turned around and was looking at the

monitors, especially the one that showed the giant monster.

"We might want to get going," the troll said.

"Yeah," Billy agreed, glancing at his watch. "We've got less than a half hour before General Bludangutts uses the O.M.G. and—"

"Oh my," the goblin said with a gulp.

Billy looked up from his watch to see that both his friends were standing before the monitors.

"What's the matter now?" he asked, and seeing what they saw, Billy gulped too.

They did indeed have to work very quickly.

Zis-Boom-Bah was awake and on the move.

Billy wasn't sure if he'd ever moved that fast before.

He tried to remember as he zoomed from the Roost on one of the bright yellow Owlcycles, zipping down the twisty-turny city streets on his way to police headquarters.

It was as if he'd drunk a whole six-pack of Zap cola.

As soon as he'd seen that Zis-Boom-Bah was awake, he'd started running. Archebold and Halifax had been right behind him. They'd jumped into the elevator, gone up to the garage and immediately gone to work.

Halifax had shown Billy where the Owlcycles were

kept, while Archebold had gone about getting the Owl-blimp inflated. It had been pretty impressive seeing the huge aircraft inflating in the sky over the open canopy of the Roost, and Billy wished he could've stayed to see it fully blown up, but he had to get to the police station and see a cop about a shrink gun.

Before the time allotted to him by the bulldog general ran out.

He had wished his pals good luck and started the powerful engine of the Owlcycle by turning a key on the handlebars. Revving the engine, he'd given them the thumbs-up, then steered the cycle toward the exit, careful not to lose his balance and tip over. Billy kept reminding himself as he drove that it was just like riding a normal bike, only this one was louder and had a motor.

So far he was doing pretty well except that the vibration of the cycle engine made him feel like he had to pee.

Billy arrived at police headquarters in record time, bringing the motorcycle to a screeching stop that he was sure made him seem much cooler than he actually was.

Leaving the bike on its side in the street—*who in their right mind would steal Owlboy's Owlcycle?*—Billy ran up the stairs into the police station.

"I need to see Chief Bloodwart right away!" Billy cried as he pushed through the doors. Monster cops stopped short as they saw him, and the racket of the station was tuned down to a murmuring buzz.

"What seems to be the problem, Owlboy?" Chief Bloodwart asked, striding out of an office at the back of the station. In hand he had a huge mug that seemed to be made from the same rocky substance that he was. "Besides the fact that we're about to be stomped into oblivion by a giant monster."

"That's why I'm here, Chief," Billy said, marching over to the police chief. "I'm going to need a pretty big favor."

"Go on," the rock monster said, taking a big slurp from his rock cup.

"Remember that shrink gun I took away from Dr. Bug and told you to lock up?"

The chief nodded. It sounded like two cinder blocks being rubbed together.

"Well, I was wondering if I could borrow it."

The chief dropped his mug and it shattered on the floor at Billy's feet. As they bent to pick up the pieces, Billy explained his plan.

"I should lock you up for coming up with an insane plan like that," the chief grumbled, wiping his large stone hands on the front of his pants. "But I have to admit, it's crazy enough to work."

The chief headed downstairs to the evidence room, Billy close behind. They unlocked the multiple locks to the special-evidence vault and then Billy had it: Dr. Bug's shrink gun.

Billy held the powerful weapon in his hand and felt a little bit afraid.

"So, you think you know how to use that?" Bloodwart asked.

"I'm sure I can figure it out," Billy said. "But I should probably talk to the doctor just to be on the safe side."

"You're in luck," the chief said, leading him from the evidence room. "The doctor is still a guest here at the station. Seems they had some bus trouble at Beelzebub Prison and couldn't get over to pick him up."

"At least something seems to have gone my way today," Billy said as he followed the chief to another set of steps and the two began their descent even farther beneath the station house.

"This is where we keep the bad ones," Bloodwart said. "The ones so nasty that I don't even want to look at them."

They walked down a long hall filled with empty jail cells except for the last. Dr. Bug sat on his bunk, wearing his loose-fitting human suit, staring out through the bars at them.

"You're not very nice," Dr. Bug scolded the chief.

"Not the first time I've heard that," the rock creature

growled. "If you know what's good for you, you'll answer Owlboy's questions without a lot of guff."

"Questions?" the doctor asked almost gleefully, his buggy eyes twinkling behind the baggy mask of his human being costume. "What kind of questions would the champion of Monstros City have for little old me?"

The villain rose from his cot and approached the bars. The mouth of the mask that Dr. Bug wore was all twisted and crazy, and Billy guessed that the bug face underneath was probably trying to smile.

Gross.

Billy held up the shrink gun for the doctor to see.

"I was wondering if you could give me some pointers on how to use this right," Billy said.

Dr. Bug giggled—at least, Billy guessed it was a giggle. It sounded like a hive of angry hornets that had been whacked with a stick.

"You want *me* to tell you how to use my deadliest device?" he asked incredulously.

"Yeah," Billy said, inspecting the weapon from all sides. "I was kind of hoping you would. It's sort of important and I'd hate to break it or screw something up really bad."

Dr. Bug stepped back from the bars, clapping his hands, and began to laugh evilly.

"Priceless," he buzzed. "You actually need me for

something." The insect tossed his head back and laughed harder. "It appears that *I*—Dr. Bug—have the upper hand at last!"

He was in the middle of laughing like a complete maniac again when Billy hit a button on the gun that he shouldn't have, and the gun was pointed right at Dr. Bug.

PZZZZAAAP!

The gun fired a beam of strangely colored light. It hit the doctor squarely in the chest, and the bug man was gone.

Or was he?

"You disintegrated him!" Chief Bloodwart exclaimed.

Billy was ready to believe him when he happened to glance down at the floor of the cell.

"No, I didn't," Billy said, pointing through the bars. "I just shrunk him."

Dr. Bug was no bigger than an inch, jumping up and down in fury. They could tell that he was screaming something, but had to lean in very close to the bars to make it out.

"That wasn't a very nice thing to do!" Dr. Bug yelled.

Billy just shrugged, again examining the buttons and knobs on the shrink gun.

"Told you I needed help working it."

CHAPTER ELEVEN

Billy was on the move again. Crouched behind the handlebars of the Owlcycle, with Dr. Bug's shrink gun hanging from his utility belt, he was on his way to the Frightening Forest.

It didn't take long for Dr. Bug to give him a tutorial on using his shrink gun. All Billy and the chief had to do was threaten to flush Dr. Bug down the toilet. (The idea had been Billy's, and Chief Bloodwart had complimented him on his tough-guy tactics.)

On the outskirts of Monstros, Billy left the main road, heading onto a snaking dirt road that would eventually bring him into the Frightening Forest. The road soon became undrivable. Billy was forced to leave the Owlcycle and make the rest of his way on foot.

It wasn't long before he heard the sound of powerful machine engines, followed by the blustery voice of the general screaming out orders to his soldiers. Curious to see what was going on, Billy started to run.

Emerging from the woods into a clearing, Billy narrowly avoided being run over by one of the army guys driving a huge truck. The truck was pulling a flatbed. Something large and covered in a tarp was strapped to it.

"What's going on?" Billy yelled over the roar of the truck engine.

Professor Carapace and General Bludangutts were standing to the side, directing the truck toward what looked like a new road cut through the Frightening Forest. Bludangutts raised his hand, stopping the truck's progress.

"Hope I'm not too late," Billy said, fingering the shrink gun. "Took me a little bit longer than I expected to come up with a plan, but I think I've got a wicked good one."

"Doesn't matter now," Bludangutts said, shaking his head. His jowls flapped loosely from side to side, flecks of spittle flying off in opposite directions. "We've already put Operation O.M.G. into effect."

"What do you mean?" Billy whined. "You said that I had two hours to come up with something to stop Zis-Boom-Bah without having to use the O.M.G."

He pulled down the sleeve of his glove again to look at his watch. "And I've still got ten minutes and twenty seconds."

"Professor Carapace and I conferred, and we determined that the O.M.G. is the only way to go. Sorry, kid."

The praying mantis scientist nodded in agreement, making his black toupee go crooked on top of his triangle-shaped head.

"I know that you're a superhero and supposed to be hot stuff, but the giant monster is on the move again, and we just can't take a chance of it going for a stroll through downtown Monstros. Now, be a good little superhero and step back so that the experts can take care of things."

General Bludangutts pushed Billy away and gestured for the truck to start moving again.

"But I've got a really good plan!" Billy yelled over the roar of the engine. "And besides, isn't using the O.M.G. dangerous for Monstros?"

Professor Carapace came running at him. "How dare you say such a thing? The O.M.G. is perfectly safe. Our testing showed that only eight detonations out of ten resulted in the total loss of life and the total destruction of all standing structures."

Billy couldn't believe what he was hearing. "Those are terrible odds," he said.

"Yes, but we're almost guaranteed victory over our enemies," the professor exclaimed, raising one of his funky clawed limbs. "And that's what matters most."

"Personally, I think that a victory where everybody stays alive and the city isn't destroyed is the way to go," Billy suggested.

Professor Carapace studied him coolly. "What would you know about it? You've only been a hero for a short period of time. You should do what the general has asked of you and step out of the way."

With those words, the professor spun around to join General Bludangutts as he directed the truck down the new road.

They were ignoring Billy now. If there was one thing that really ticked him off, it was being ignored.

"*Hey!*" Billy yelled at the top of his lungs.

The general, the professor and the soldiers standing around all looked in his direction.

"*Don't you even want to hear what my plan is?*" he asked.

Bludangutts rolled his watery eyes and then motioned for the truck to cut its engine.

"Fine," the bulldog creature growled. "Why don't you tell us your special plan as quickly as you can so that we can get back to the job of destroying our enemy before he can destroy us?"

Billy unhooked Dr. Bug's shrink gun from his belt.

"I really do appreciate this," he told them. He then motioned for all the soldiers standing around to come closer. "I worked really hard on this plan and I'd like all of you to hear."

"Get on with it, kid," Bludangutts grumbled.

"But, General, the killing and the destruction . . . ," Professor Carapace whined.

"It can wait a little bit longer," the general said. "And besides, it will make the victory taste all the sweeter."

Billy knew that no matter what, he couldn't let them set off the O.M.G. He had come up with another plan. He almost hated to do it, but they didn't leave him any choice. Monstros City was his to protect, and he wasn't about to let anybody do anything bad to it.

"We're waiting, Owlboy," General Bludangutts said as he crossed his arms.

"Sure," Billy said. He held up the shrink gun. "I was going to use this."

Professor Carapace let out a laugh. "That puny thing is going to stop Zis-Boom-Bah?" he scoffed. "I think maybe somebody needs to have his hero's license revoked."

The soldiers and the general all started to laugh.

Billy made up his mind at that point that he *really*

didn't care for Professor Carapace. Suddenly he didn't feel at all bad about what he was going to do.

"Yeah, I know it's not as spiffy as your O.M.G. bomb," Billy said.

Grinning, the professor ran over to the flatbed and tore away the cover to reveal the explosive device beneath.

The O.M.G. was about the size of Billy's mother's washing machine, but it was round, with all these crazy-looking spikes sticking out of it. It sort of reminded him of one of the old Christmas ornaments his folks had saved from the trees they'd had when they were kids.

"Now, *that's* a weapon," Professor Carapace buzzed.

"Can't argue with that," Billy said as the professor came back to join them. "But I was going to use this to stop Zis-Boom-Bah." Billy waved the shrink gun around.

"What's it do?" General Bludangutts asked.

"It's a shrink gun," Billy explained, starting to fiddle with some of the knobs and buttons. "It shoots a shrink ray."

"A shrink ray?" Professor Carapace asked. "So it shrinks things?"

"Yep," Billy said as he pointed the weapon at them all. "All I have to do is point it at the monster and fire."

Billy pulled the trigger, and a wide band of energy blasted from the weapon to engulf the general, Carapace, the soldiers, the military vehicles, including the truck pulling the O.M.G., and the O.M.G. itself.

FZZZZAP!

"Whoops! Look what I've done," Billy said.

He walked over to the shrunken soldiers, careful not to step on them. The general was squeaking bloody murder, as was the professor, but Billy just pretended not to hear them.

"I'm really sorry about this, guys," he said, heading toward the path that he was sure would bring him pretty close to Zis-Boom-Bah's current location. "I promise that I'll be back as quick as I can to figure out how to return you guys to your normal size."

As Billy walked past the tiny truck, he glanced down at the shrunk O.M.G. device. Now it *definitely* looked like one of his parents' ornaments.

"And since you're all tiny now, it looks as though it's going to be up to me to save the day," he said, heading down the path with the shrink gun in hand. "Oh well. A superhero's gotta do what a superhero's gotta do."

Behind him, the general's squeal of anger became even louder.

Looking up through the trees, Billy spotted the bright yellow Owlblimp as it floated in the sky.

Suddenly a sound like a lion's roar, only a bazillion

times louder, filled the air. Billy realized that Zis-Boom-Bah must be close by.

A few seconds later, he reached an area of the forest that looked as though it had been hit by the grandfather of all tornados: the growth overturned, trees broken into toothpicks. And standing in the midst of all that destruction was the fearsome beast called Zis-Boom-Bah.

The monster was watching the Owlblimp as it floated through the sky in a circle. As Billy carefully moved closer, a hatch opened beneath the canopy of the aircraft, and from it, a multitude of snack products rained down.

Zis-Boom-Bah reached out to capture some, then sniffed the huge handful. His eyes widened and the antennae on top of his apelike head wiggled around excitedly, and he tossed the handful into his enormous maw.

"YUMMMM!" the monster roared, bending down to snatch a few hundred pounds more of tasty treats. Still more fell from the belly of the Owlblimp.

Billy crept closer, trying to remember what Dr. Bug had told him about the various controls on the shrink gun.

Zis-Boom-Bah began to roar, and Billy looked away from his weapon to see what the matter was.

The Owlblimp had stopped dropping treats.

Can they be out of snacks already? Billy wondered.

The monster bellowed again, stomping his dinosaur feet and clenching his fists in rage. Zis-Boom-Bah shook those fists at the Owlblimp, as if telling it to start the snack delivery pronto, or there was gonna be trouble.

And trouble there was.

Billy had started to creep even closer, crawling over the fallen trees and the piles of overturned earth to get to the monster so that he could use the shrink gun on him, when it happened.

As the Owlblimp came around the great beast again, Zis-Boom-Bah suddenly jumped into the air, grabbing the dirigible and pulling it down from the sky.

"Oh my gosh!" Billy screamed. He could see up into the Owlblimp's gondola, and the shapes of Archebold and Halifax were being thrown around like beans inside a maraca.

Billy knew that it was time to act. He rechecked the controls on the shrink gun and ran toward the huge clawed feet of Zis-Boom-Bah. He aimed Dr. Bug's weapon, finger tensed on the trigger, and prepared himself for the multicolored miniaturizing light.

Just as he was about to pull the trigger, the toe of his right boot caught on a gnarled root sticking up from the ground.

Billy let out a yelp of surprise, and as he fell forward, the shrink gun flew from his hand.

Only one thing went through his mind: *Don't break. Don't break. Don't break. Don't break. Don't break. Don't break. . . .*

He hit the ground, all the while keeping his eyes on the shrink gun. His face twisted up in pain as he watched the gun descend, about to hit the dirt.

Please don't break. Please don't break. Please don't break. Please . . .

The shrink gun hit the ground and went off, a blinding flash of light shooting out from the barrel of the weapon and hitting Billy right in the face.

It all happened so fast that he didn't even have a chance to duck. There was an explosion of color before his eyes, and suddenly he felt as though he were riding up in an elevator—only this one was going about a million miles an hour.

Billy felt himself come to a sudden stop, his stomach winding up somewhere near his face. He stumbled around a bit, trying to get his balance back, and as his eyes began to focus, he realized that he was looking straight ahead at Zis-Boom-Bah, who was holding on to the Owlblimp.

Looking straight ahead, eye to eye with the great monster.

Billy quickly glanced down at himself, and at the forest beneath him, realizing what had happened.

He was now as big as Zis-Boom-Bah.

The discharge of the shrink gun had enlarged him. And the monster seemed pretty darned excited.

At least there's one good thing about being the same size as Zis-Boom-Bah, Billy thought as the monster, excited to see another giant creature standing in front of him, released the Owlblimp, letting it float back up into the sky.

"Oh boy," Billy said, fighting the urge to freak out. He was certain that this could lead to only one thing: a superbattle between Owlboy and the terror that was Zis-Boom-Bah.

He watched the Owlblimp climbing higher into the sky and saw Halifax and Archebold waving crazily from the windows.

"Get down to the ground and find Dr. Bug's shrink gun," Billy called out, cupping his hand over his mouth. His voice was like the roar of a jet engine. He could see his pals covering their ears in the gondola below the Owlblimp.

"You've got to get me back to my normal size," he added, using more of a whisper. He didn't want Halifax and Archebold to be deafened by his orders.

They must've known the importance of what he was

asking of them, because almost immediately the Owl-blimp started to descend toward a safer part of the Frightening Forest.

Billy turned back to his bigger problem and saw that the monster was glaring at him evilly, baring his huge sharp-looking teeth in what might have been a crazy smile. Billy wasn't sure if he'd ever seen so many teeth in one mouth before. The tooth fairy would be filing for bankruptcy if only half of those choppers were to fall out.

"Stay calm," Billy said softly, holding out his hands toward the monster. "Be a good giant ape-bug-fish-dinosaur thing, okay?"

Zis-Boom-Bah let out a weird kind of bark, which caused Billy to jump.

The monster then looked around himself, letting out what could only have been a squeal of delight as he apparently found what he was looking for.

"Hey, what are you up to?" Billy asked as the monster picked up a boulder, pulling it from where it had probably rested for many years.

"That's a pretty good-sized rock there," he said. "Hope you're not thinking of doing with that what I think you're thinking about doing with that."

Zis-Boom-Bah tossed the boulder at him, doing exactly what Billy thought the giant monster was going to do. Billy stepped out of the way of the flying rock, watching as it crashed into a section of trees. It took them out like a bowling ball knocking down pins at the Lucky Strike Bowling Alley.

"You better knock it off," Billy warned, wagging a finger at the beast.

Zis-Boom-Bah just seemed to become more amused, turning around, his fish tail wagging excitedly from side to side as he looked for something else. The monster pounced on an even bigger rock, this one partially covered with a thick growth of bushes and trees. With a grunt, Zis-Boom-Bah hauled the enormous stone from the ground and turned back to Billy. His eyes twinkled mischievously as the buglike antennae moved around on top of his head.

"I'm warning you," Billy said, raising his voice. "You better not—"

The monster threw this one at him too.

The rock zoomed right past his head and Billy was reminded of being at school, ducking one of Randy Kulkowski's killer dodgeball throws.

It almost seems like he's playing, Billy thought. *But that's crazy. Or is it?*

Zis-Boom-Bah stood there, watching Billy with wide, eager eyes. It reminded Billy of something, and it took a minute for him to realize what.

The way the monster was standing—staring—it was almost like a dog wanting to play catch.

Billy decided that he had to try something before the monster tossed another mountain at him.

He turned to where the first of the boulders thrown at him had landed. He bent down and strained to pick it up, then turned back to Zis-Boom-Bah.

"Is this what you want?" Billy asked him.

The monster's eyes grew round with excitement as his fish tail swished back and forth faster and faster.

Using all his Owlboy superstrength, Billy threw the boulder toward Zis-Boom-Bah, careful not to hit the beast.

The mighty rock sailed over Zis-Boom-Bah's head and the monster immediately went to retrieve it, just like Kristy Bratton's Labrador going after a tennis ball.

Billy had been right: Zis-Boom-Bah wasn't attacking; he was just *playing*!

"Good . . . monster," Billy said, not sure what to say to the beast as he returned with the boulder Billy had just thrown. "You don't want to hurt anybody, do you? You're just lonely, looking for somebody your own size to—"

Zis-Boom-Bah roared with joy as he threw the rock, and this time Billy wasn't quite fast enough to get out of the way.

"Ouff!" Billy said, catching the projectile in the chest. The wind was knocked from his lungs as he flipped backward to the ground.

The monster leaped about happily on his T. rex legs, waving his gorilla arms in the air, doing a bizarre kind of monster dance.

"Nice," Billy said, rolling the rock from his chest before climbing to his feet.

Zis-Boom-Bah finished with his dance and was already looking for another rock.

Billy's mind was racing as he tried to think of what to do next—not wanting to get hit with another pitch from the playful beast—when he was suddenly struck by a beam of multicolored light.

It felt as though he were now coming down in an elevator from the millionth floor. As the bizarre light show began to fade, and the nauseating dizziness started to pass, Billy saw his friends standing there.

"How's that?" Halifax asked, holding Dr. Bug's shrink gun.

"Good, I think," Archebold answered, giving Billy a careful look over.

"I think he might've been a little shorter," Halifax said, aiming the weapon at Billy again.

Billy lunged at the pair. "I'm fine," he said, snatching the weapon away from the troll before something bad happened.

A horrible moan filled the air, freezing them all in their tracks.

"You're fine, but *he* isn't," Archebold said, looking up over the tree line at Zis-Boom-Bah.

The monster was cradling his newest rock, head tossed back as he howled to the night sky.

"He's probably sad because I'm gone," Billy said.

"Sad because you're gone?" Halifax repeated. "Sad because he didn't rip your head off is more like it."

"You're wrong about him," Billy said, watching the beast. "He isn't mean or bad at all; he's just lonely and looking for somebody to play with."

"I think one of those boulders must have hit you in the head," the troll said, twirling one of his sausage-sized fingers at the side of his shaggy head.

"No, really," Billy said. "Didn't you see us playing with the rocks?"

"I saw what appeared to be a superbattle of mighty behemoths," Halifax said.

Billy looked to Archebold. "And you?"

"I saw a unique display of interpretive dance."

Billy and Halifax just stared at the goblin, who shrugged.

Zis-Boom-Bah wailed again, and Billy thought it was one of the saddest sounds he'd ever heard. It was the sound of someone—or some*thing*—who had lost something very special.

Billy had a sudden crazy thought about the cranky

199

old man at Shady Acres. Could that be his problem as well—that he didn't have any friends and might have lost someone who was important?

It was something to think about, but he had bigger fish to fry at the moment.

"He's very upset that I'm gone," Billy said.

Zis-Boom-Bah was getting angry and tossed his rock down onto the ground. The rock hit and the ground did a little dance, the force of the impact sending a vibration so strong through the earth that it tossed Billy and his friends into the air as if they were on a trampoline.

"So, do you mind sharing what you plan on doing about that?" Archebold asked, helping a dazed-looking Halifax up from the ground.

"What I had planned to do earlier," Billy said, adjusting the knobs on the shrink gun. "I'm gonna shrink my problem down to a more manageable size."

It looked as though Zis-Boom-Bah was about to lose it completely, his gorilla arms tossed up into the air, his mouth—filled with row upon row of nasty teeth—open in a roar of anger tinged with sadness.

Billy ran through the trees to get closer. He aimed Dr. Bug's shrink gun up at the monster and pulled the trigger, a beam of rainbow light erupting from the barrel of the weapon to strike one of the giant's knees.

The colorful energy spread up and eventually all

over the monster's huge body, and like magic, he appeared to be gone.

But Billy knew otherwise, looking down at the ground for his results.

Zis-Boom-Bah had been shrunk to the size of one of Billy's action figures. The monster tossed his head back and roared, but it came out sounding like a mouse squeak.

"Hey there, fella," Billy said, squatting down in front of the now tiny monster. Zis-Boom-Bah seemed glad to see him, his fish tail wagging like a happy puppy's.

Billy held out his hand, and the monster jumped into his palm. "There ya go; that's a good monster."

"He seems sort of cute when he's not trying to step on you," Archebold said, holding out his hand so that Zis-Boom-Bah could sniff it.

"Like I said, I don't think he was trying to hurt anybody," Billy explained. "I think he was just trying to find some friends his own size."

"I still don't trust him," Halifax said, sticking his own finger in front of Zis-Boom-Bah's face for a sniff.

The monster bit down into the troll's finger as if it were an all-beef frank.

"YEOOWCH!" Halifax screeched, pulling his hand back. "I told you he was still dangerous."

"He's not dangerous; he's probably just hungry. I

know I am." Billy remembered that he hadn't had anything to eat for a while. "We'll take him back to the Roost with us and we'll all have a snack."

Billy unsnapped one of the pouches on his utility belt and dropped Zis-Boom-Bah inside. "I'll just put you in here for safekeeping."

"Let's hope that the army guys don't decide to search your pouches," Archebold said with a laugh. "Wouldn't they get a surprise?"

Suddenly Billy froze.

"Oh crap, I just remembered."

"What, did you leave the iron on?" Halifax asked.

"No, I just remembered that I had to shrink General Bludangutts and the Monstros City Defense Corps down to miniature size so that I could take care of this problem."

"Cool!" Archebold and Halifax said at the same time.

"Well, now I've got to go and return them to normal."

"Are you sure?" Archebold asked.

Billy nodded, as much as he didn't want to.

Entering the clearing in the Frightening Forest where Billy thought he'd left the general and his soldiers,

Billy, Archebold and Halifax were careful where they stepped, not wanting to accidentally squish any of the tiny army guys.

"There they are," Archebold said, pointing to the far end of the clearing. Beneath a particularly scary gnarled and twisted old tree, the general and his men had lined up a row of upchucks—the monstrous equivalent of woodchucks, only these threw up—and were attempting to draft them into service in their army.

"They sure know how to make friends," Archebold said with a disgusted shake of his head.

"Are you sure you've got to put them back the way they were?" Halifax asked. "They're awfully cute this size."

"Don't tempt me," Billy said with a sigh, unhooking the shrink gun from his belt and checking that the settings were all right.

He made sure that the general, his men and most of their vehicles were within range; then he set the beam of Dr. Bug's shrink gun for extra-wide so that he would hit them all in the first shot.

"Here goes nothing," Billy said, taking aim.

FZZZZAP!

Spots danced before Billy's eyes, and then the clearing was crowded with army guys, their jeeps and trucks and a very angry-looking General Bludangutts.

"Hey," Billy said with a wave. "Told ya I'd be back to make you big again."

The general snorted loudly and stomped toward him, anger burning in his beady little eyes. Professor Carapace came to join them.

"Do you have any idea what you've done, hero?" the general growled. "The danger to lives and property you've likely caused?"

"If you're talking about the Zis-Boom-Bah problem, sir, I've got that completely under control."

The general looked as though he'd been slapped in the face with a fresh fish.

"What sort of nonsense are you spewing, hero?" he asked.

"This is not the time for humor, bird-boy," the professor added. "We'll barely have the proper amount of time to activate the O.M.G."

"He told you that's been taken care of," Archebold said, coming to stand beside Billy.

"Without any devastating damage to the population, or the city, I might add." Halifax proudly put his arm around Billy's shoulder.

Bludangutts studied Billy carefully. "Let me get this right," he said. "You're saying that the problem that existed with the giant monster Zis-Boom-Bah has been taken care of . . . that no threat exists any longer?"

Billy nodded. "That's what I'm saying."

Zis-Boom-Bah started to move around in his utility belt pouch and Billy almost let out a yelp. He brought his hands down quickly to his side, giving the pouch a gentle smack.

"That's impossible," Carapace screeched. "We calculated that there was no other way to defeat our enemy besides the O.M.G."

"Well, I guess you calculated wrong, Carapace, old boy," Halifax said, nudging Archebold with his elbow. The goblin chuckled.

"This can't be true," the general growled. He extended his arm and snapped his fingers. Like magic, one of his soldiers appeared, handing a large walkie-talkie to the general.

Bludangutts brought the communication device to his ear. "This is General Bludangutts in the field; please clarify current situation in regard to enemy Zis-Boom-Bah."

Static crackled briefly before a voice began to speak.

"Threat has been neutralized, sir," the voice on the other end said. "Headquarters states that it's time for you to gather up your toys and come home."

Billy could have sworn he saw two miniature explosions go off in the general's pupils.

"How can this be?" the general asked.

"Guess I'm better at being a hero than you thought," Billy answered.

"And the beast's remains? Is there a body?"

"Nope, no body," Billy said, laying his hand on top of the pouch at his side to hide its movement. "Guess he was just shrunk down into nothingness."

The general looked as if he had gone into shock, staring off into the distance.

Suddenly there was a horrible scream and they all turned to see Professor Carapace coming toward them, holding something in his claws.

"My beautiful weapon," he said, tears dribbling from his compound eyes. "My beautiful, deadly O.M.G."

He was holding the miniaturized truck and trailer with the tiny O.M.G. strapped on the back. Billy purposely hadn't brought it back to its original size.

"You have to make it big again," the insect professor demanded.

"Sorry," Billy said with a shrug. "The battery's dead on this thing." He pretended to pull the trigger on the shrink gun, showing Carapace that nothing happened. "See? As soon as I charge the battery, I'll give you a call. We can do lunch, or maybe go out for a Frappuccino or something."

Not wanting to wait around for any further problems to spring up, Billy and the gang bid their farewells to the Monstros City Defense Corps and ran as quickly as they could to the waiting Owlblimp.

They couldn't get back to the Roost fast enough.

CHAPTER TWELVE

Billy carefully took a bite of his tasty treat, the tentacles of the fried cephalopod on a stick delicately breaking off in his mouth.

"This is melt-in-your-mouth cephalopod," he said, chewing the somewhat rubbery fried appendage. "It was awful nice of Sammy's Snacks to send these over to us."

Halifax was on his fourth cephalopod, dunking it in some yellowish green dipping sauce, which looked like something squeezed out of an infected leg wound, before eating the entire thing in one enormous bite.

"We saved his butt," Halifax said, his mouth stuffed with fried octopod goodness. "If it weren't for us, he'd still have an entire warehouse full of snacks on the verge of going rotten."

"Isn't it awesome when a plan comes together?" Billy asked, breaking off a tentacle and giving the piece of fried treat to the tiny Zis-Boom-Bah, who waited patiently on the edge of the snack-room table.

"Here ya go, Zis," Billy said as the miniaturized monster took the offered piece of food and began to eat it eagerly. "Hey, look. Zis likes fried cephalopod too."

"Can't imagine there's much he won't eat," Halifax said, momentarily looking at his finger where the tiny monster had bitten him earlier. "So, what are we going to do with him?"

Billy shrugged, wiping his greasy face on a napkin before reaching into the box for another fried treat. "I don't know. He seems pretty happy this size, so I was thinking he might be cool to keep around here . . . like a mascot."

An octopod stopped midway to the troll's mouth.

"You're not serious."

"Why not?" Billy asked. "You guys have plenty of room here, and plenty to eat—not that he would eat much now, anyway; he's so small. I think he would fit in quite nicely."

Halifax scowled at the tiny creature who watched him from the table. "I don't know; he still could get into lots of trouble."

"Well, you and Archebold will just have to keep an

eye on him," Billy said. "Besides, what else are we going to do with him? Remember, he's all alone, and we're his friends now."

The image of the cranky old man from Shady Acres again popped into Billy's head. He wondered if that could be the reason the old man was so mean. Maybe he lost all his friends so long ago that he didn't remember how to have them anymore.

"I guess he won't be too much of a bother," Halifax said. The troll again presented his finger to the tiny terror, and again was bitten.

"YARRRGH!" Halifax screamed, tearing his finger away. "Did you see that? He almost ate me alive!"

Billy just shook his head as he finished up his last fried cephalopod on a stick. "When are you going to learn to keep your finger out of his mouth?" he said.

Archebold came into the room, talking on a portable phone.

"I think a parade would be a wonderful idea," the goblin said, reaching into the box for a fried snack. "Give me a minute and I'll see if he's free."

Archebold put a hand over the phone. "It's the mayor of Monstros and he wants to give you a parade for saving the city from Zis-Boom-Bah. Are you interested?"

"Sure," Billy said with a growing smile. "A parade for me—who'da thunk it?"

"He says a parade would be a real honor," Archebold said, getting back on the phone. "Why don't you give us a few nights to rest up and we'll get back to you about when it would be most convenient?"

Zis-Boom-Bah started to howl from the table, wanting some of Archebold's fried treat.

The goblin put his finger up to his mouth, shushing the tiny beast. "That would be great, Mayor," he said. "So we'll give you a ringy-dingy in a few nights. That's right. Love to the missus. Buh-bye."

He pushed a button, hanging up the phone.

"If you weren't popular before, you sure will be after the parade," Archebold said proudly, taking a bite of his cephalopod. "This is gonna be great."

He broke off a tentacle and tossed it to Zis-Boom-Bah.

"We're gonna keep him," Billy said. "As the Roost's mascot . . . Is that all right?"

The goblin thought for a minute. "Sure, I can't see any problem with that. He'll make a great addition to our security system."

"He doesn't try to eat *you* every time you try to make friends," Halifax grumbled from the corner, where he'd gone to mope.

"Keep your fingers out of his mouth," Archebold said.

"That's what I've been telling him," Billy said,

getting out of his seat and stretching. "Well, I think that's enough superheroing for me right now."

"Is it that time already?" Archebold asked, looking at his watch.

"Yeah, think I'm gonna head back and spend some time with my aunt Tilley before she has to go back to her apartment."

"Are you sure you want to do that?" Archebold asked. He looked surprised.

Billy gently patted Zis-Boom-Bah's tiny gorilla head as he got ready to leave. "Yeah, I think I do," he said. He remembered the conversation he'd had with the old woman before it was interrupted by a goblin dressed as a little girl knocking on the door.

And he found that he didn't mind the idea of going home at all.

In fact, after all the craziness he had been through in Monstros, he was kind of looking forward to it.

The long weekend was practically at an end.

Billy had returned home from Monstros, crawling up the winding passage and out the top of the stone coffin within the Sprylock family mausoleum. He'd quickly changed his clothes, shoving his Owlboy costume into his backpack, before heading home.

No matter how many times he experienced it, Billy was always amazed at the whole passage-of-time thing when it came to Monstros and the real world. Although his head was filled with at least a day's worth of memories, in the real world barely any time had passed at all.

He'd had all of Sunday to spend with his aunt and his family, and it was kind of nice not to be doing battle with some slimy giant supervillain who wanted to steal stuff, destroy stuff or just be nasty for the sake of being nasty.

He needed a little break after the last adventure, a little downtime to recharge the batteries before heading back to his second home in the city of monsters.

Sunday had been just what he was looking for: a day filled with stuff he normally would have considered boring. On that day, it was perfectly fine with him. His focus had been his aunt and trying to spend as much time with her as possible. Always at the back of his mind was what he had figured out about Zis-Boom-Bah during his last Owlboy adventure: that being alone and not having any friends could transform you into something not so nice.

He never wanted his aunt Tilley to feel that way.

Sunday had been filled with shopping—Aunt Tilley needing some new unmentionables, whatever the heck those were—and a nice lunch at Luigi's downtown.

They'd even let Billy run into the Hero's Hovel to say hello to Cole and Claudius, and to pick up some new reading material.

All in all, it had been a pretty awesome day, and Billy didn't miss superheroing in Monstros one little bit.

Well, maybe a little bit.

Aunt Tilley's last night at the house had been just as pleasant. They'd had a nice dinner of spaghetti and meatballs. Dad had made his special sauce, which, according to Mom, he hadn't done in a long, long time, and then they'd had dessert and played some games. Their build-a-Transmogrifier-to-conquer-the-universe game had been a success, and Billy had been quite impressed with the killer robot his aunt had designed to win the game.

They'd all gone in to watch TV to wind down for the night, and discovered that a special edition of *Polkaing with the Famous* was on. They all watched the special presentation without falling asleep, and Billy found that he sort of liked the show, once he figured out the rules, and decided that maybe he might even watch it again sometime.

Well, at least when his aunt came to visit.

*   *   *

Aunt Tilley wanted to get back to her apartment as soon as she could on Monday, so Mom had gotten up early and had made them all a big breakfast.

The smell of some kind of meat cooking—it reminded Billy of the smell of something called belcher beef, which the street vendors in Monstros sold from carts, but he doubted that his mother was cooking that down in the kitchen—got him out of bed and dressed.

But before Billy went downstairs to have a bite to eat, there was something he wanted to do. He had a theory to test out on the cranky old man at Shady Acres. He went through a few of the comic book storage boxes in his closet, finding some particularly cool issues of different titles, and stuck a good-sized stack inside his book bag to bring with him when they brought his aunt back to her apartment later that morning.

Breakfast was good. He had been right about it not being belcher beef; it turned out to be Canadian bacon.

With breakfast finished, they cleaned up and were soon loading Aunt Tilley's things into the car as they prepared to make the journey back to Shady Acres.

"There's that cute little girl who came by yesterday," Aunt Tilley said, waving to Victoria, who was seated on her Princess Big Wheel at the end of her driveway. She waved back enthusiastically, breaking out into a song she must've learned at school about a little lost ladybug.

Billy didn't have the heart to tell his aunt that it wasn't Victoria she'd met the day before but his goblin sidekick disguised as a little girl.

He doubted she would believe him anyway.

"She seems much cuter today than yesterday," Aunt Tilley mused as they pulled out and drove up the street and away from the house. "The lighting must be bad in the kitchen."

The trip to Shady Acres seemed longer than the last time, but eventually they arrived. Billy helped his mom and dad carry Aunt Tilley's things into the building, up in the elevator and to her door.

Aunt Tilley excitedly let herself in and seemed really happy with the persimmon color of her walls—whatever the heck persimmon was. It looked like orange to Billy.

He and Dad hauled her stuff into the apartment next, the smell of fresh paint heavy in the air, and while his mom and dad got her settled back in, he asked if he could go down to the recreation room and get another look at that fifty-inch plasma TV.

His dad said sure, and told him to be back in around a half hour.

Billy ran to the elevator, book bag slung over his shoulder, and was soon descending to the seventh floor. The corridors leading to the recreation room were empty, and he wasn't sure if he was going to find the person he was looking for.

He entered the room to darkness. The shades had yet to be pulled open, and the television had yet to be turned on. Billy was about to leave, disappointed that he wasn't going to get a chance to try out his theory, when he realized that he wasn't alone.

Cranky Old Man was sitting at the back of the room, by himself at a table, nursing a cup of coffee in a Styrofoam cup.

Billy cleared his throat, but there was no response from the guy.

Billy walked over to one of the windows, grabbed a cord and drew the curtains open, allowing beams of sunlight to spill into the room.

"What the heck are you doing that for?" the cranky old man complained from his seat. "Can't you see that some of us like it dark in here? . . . It's too gosh darn bright."

"Can't see to read without some kind of light," Billy said, going to the table the cranky guy was sitting at.

"What do you gotta read here for? Why don't you go to a library or something?" Cranky Old Man growled, raising his Styrofoam cup to his mouth and having himself a drink.

"Can't," Billy said simply. He unzipped his book

bag and removed his comics. "My folks are with my aunt Tilley, and I'm going to read until they're ready to go."

The old man muttered something unintelligible as Billy started to flip through the first of the comics.

"This is a good one," Billy said, staring at the artwork in the first of the pages' panels before reading the captions and the word balloons.

"Don't care," Cranky Old Man said, turning himself sideways in his chair so that he wasn't looking at Billy.

"A really good one."

"I really don't care."

Billy flipped through some more pages before he spoke again.

"Did you ever read comics when you were a kid?"

The man didn't respond at first, drinking his coffee down to the last drop. Billy knew that the man could have gone away at any time, leaving him there to read his comics, but he chose not to.

"A few," he said, finally answering. "Really wasn't big into reading."

"Too bad," Billy said. "Bet you would've read some really old ones."

The man didn't respond to that but continued with his original thought.

"I liked to build stuff," he said, turning in his seat

toward Billy. "Liked to use my hands. Bet you don't even know what I'm talking about . . . kids today with their televisions and computers."

"I build stuff all the time," Billy said, not even glancing up from his comic. "I think that's almost as fun as reading comics."

Billy looked up and smiled at the old man.

"Almost," Billy added.

The old man sort of smiled back, but it could have easily been a touch of gas.

"What's the last thing you built?" the old man asked, turning the Styrofoam cup around in his hands.

"I tried to build a robot a few weeks ago," Billy said. "But I couldn't get it to work. I think it had something to do with the fact that I didn't know how to build a computer brain."

The old man nodded slowly, as if giving it some thought.

"Could be," he said.

Billy went back to his comics, closing the one he was looking at and picking a new one from the stack.

"Any Winged Fury in that stack?" Cranky asked.

Billy shook his head. "Winged Fury? Who's that?"

"It's what I used to like when I was your age," he said. "A long, long time ago."

Billy took half the stack and slid it across the table

218

toward the old man. "No Winged Fury, but I've got these."

Cranky picked up one of the comics, studied the cover and opened the book. "Can't tell ya the last time I looked at one of these," he said.

"They're still pretty cool," Billy commented.

They both sat in silence, each of them looking at a comic book, until the old-timer suddenly spoke.

"Pete," he said, looking up from the comic.

"What?" Billy asked, unsure of what the man had just said.

"My name is Pete . . . just in case you're interested, which you're probably not." Pete looked back down at the comic and started flipping through the pages.

"Cool. I'm Billy and I'm sorry that I changed the channel you were watching a few days ago."

"Wasn't watching anything," Pete said. "I was asleep." He started to smile. "Scared ya pretty good, though."

Billy laughed. "Scared the crap out of me."

They both laughed, continuing to look through the comic books Billy had brought with him.

"These aren't anything like I remember," Pete said. "The colors are so bright, and the drawings much more detailed."

Billy agreed with a nod, feeling pretty good about his theory being right.

"And if you think those are cool, next week I'll bring you some other ones that will blow your doors right off their hinges."

Pete looked up from his comic and Billy saw that there was a smile—a real smile—on his face.

"I'd like that, Billy," he said. "I'd like that very much."

EPILOGUE

The Monarch really didn't understand why he hated Owlboy so much.

But sitting in his secret lair, deep beneath the streets of Monstros City, he watched a huge monitor shaped like a serpent's eye, and found himself growing angrier and angrier that Monstros hadn't been destroyed by Zis-Boom-Bah and that the accursed Owlboy was still alive.

The streets were filled with people celebrating the hero's victory over the giant beast that had been slowly making its way toward the city. Somehow Owlboy had stopped the giant monster's advance.

Somehow.

His anger felt like a sharp knife poking him over and

over again in his stomach. The Monstros City news broadcast showed some footage of the Owlblimp flying over the city, the young hero hanging from the basket, waving to the citizens below.

The people of Monstros loved him. Loved him almost as much as the Monarch despised him.

As much as it infuriated him, he could not take his eyes away from the television coverage. He'd been watching since they'd first made the announcement that Monstros had been saved. He had been waiting for an announcement of a different kind, one about the city being in ruin, and the final report that Owlboy had most definitely been destroyed.

But it didn't come, and now all he had to watch was this.

Klot and Mukus sniffled behind him. They had fearfully brought him the news that his plans had been thwarted by Owlboy, but he had already heard. And now they waited, likely terrified that he was going to turn his anger toward Owlboy against them.

But that would be a waste of good anger.

The Monarch turned his chair around and listened to his lackeys gasp.

"We're sorry that your plans didn't go the way you wanted," Mukus said, his bulbous body dripping to form a slimy puddle on the floor beneath him.

"Better luck next time?" Klot then said. "If at first you don't succeed, try, try again?"

The Monarch believed that the idiot was actually attempting to make him feel better.

"If life hands you dingleberries, then you make dingle—"

"Silence!" the Monarch bellowed, his booming voice echoing through the underground chamber.

"Here it comes," Mukus said, closing his eyes tightly. "It was nice knowing you, Klot."

"Right back atcha, Mukus, old pal."

The Monarch watched them shiver and shake for a bit before continuing.

"Leave me," he said with a wave of his black-gloved hand.

"You mean you're not going to kill us?" Mukus asked.

"Would you rather I destroy you completely?" the Monarch asked.

Mukus shook his head, flecks of slime flying around the chamber. "No, sir, I'd rather be very much alive."

"Me too," Klot agreed. "Being alive is much better than being dead. You smell a lot better too."

"Then go, before I change my mind," the Monarch said as he turned his chair back to the snake-eye-shaped monitor.

The lackeys scrambled quickly from the room, just in case he did have a change of heart.

And the Monarch's anger continued to escalate as he watched the continuous coverage of Owlboy's rescue of Monstros City.

It was a good anger he felt coursing through him, an anger that could be put to good use in helping him devise his next insidious scheme to destroy the new Owlboy.

Once and for all.

THOMAS E. SNIEGOSKI is a novelist and comic book scripter who has worked for every major company in the comics industry.

As a comic book writer, his work includes *Stupid, Stupid Rat Tails*, a miniseries prequel to the international hit *Bone*. He has also written tales featuring such characters as Hellboy, Batman, Daredevil, Wolverine, and the Punisher.

He is also the author of the groundbreaking quartet of teen fantasy novels entitled The Fallen, the first of which (*Fallen*) was produced as a television movie for the ABC Family Channel. *Sleeper Code* and *Sleeper Agenda*, the first two books in his Sleeper Conspiracy series, are available from Razorbill. With Christopher Golden, he is the coauthor of the dark fantasy series The Menagerie, as well as the young readers' fantasy series OutCast, optioned by Universal Pictures. Sniegoski and Golden also wrote the graphic novel *BPRD: Hollow Earth*, a spinoff of the fan favorite comic book series Hellboy.

Sniegoski was born and raised in Massachusetts,

where he still lives with his wife, LeeAnne, and their Labrador retriever, Mulder. Please visit the author at www.sniegoski.com.

ERIC POWELL is the writer and artist of the award-winning comic book series The Goon for Dark Horse Comics. He has also contributed work to such comic titles as *Arkham Asylum*, *Buffy the Vampire Slayer*, *Hellboy: Weird Tales*, *Star Wars Tales*, *The Incredible Hulk*, *MAD Magazine*, *Swamp Thing*, and *The Simpsons*.